ZANE PRESENTS

CRANBERRY WINTER

Dear Reader:

Ruth P. Watson's debut novel, *Blackberry Days of Summer*, offered readers a glimpse into African American life in Virginia post World War I. *Cranberry Winter* follows the sequel, *An Elderberry Fall*, and we find Carrie in Richmond, still married to Simon, her Colored League baseball fanatic husband who now is missing so much that questioning his whereabouts is a way of life.

Herman Camm, her womanizing stepfather who raped her and is the father of her son, was murdered. But Carrie is not totally convinced he's actually dead as she fears his twin brother, Kindred, could be him. Is this the case or is it her imagination? Throw in the local nightclub singer Pearl and a flirtatious neighbor Nadine who can't keep her eyes off Simon, and you have drama mixed with suspense.

Infidelity and trust are recurring themes in Watson's third book of historical fiction. Her next title in the series is *Strawberry Spring*, and if you haven't read how it all started, an excerpt from *Blackberry Days of Summer* appears in the back of this book. A new musical stage play, *Blackberry Daze*, co-written by the author, is based on the novel.

As always, thanks for supporting myself and the Strebor Books family. We strive to bring you the most cutting-edge, out-of-the-box material on the market. You can find me on Facebook @AuthorZane or you can email me at zane@eroticanoir.com.

Blessings,

Zane

Publisher
Strebor Books
www.simonandschuster.com

ALSO BY RUTH P. WATSON
Blackberry Days of Summer
An Elderberry Fall

ZANE PRESENTS

CRANBERRY WINTER

RUTH P. WATSON

STREBOR BOOKS

NEW YORK LONDON TORONTO SYDNEY

SBI

Strebor Books
P.O. Box 6505
Largo, MD 20792
www.simonandschuster.com

This book is a work of fiction. Names, characters, places and incidents are products of the author's imagination or are used fictitiously. Any resemblance to actual events or locales or persons, living or dead, is entirely coincidental.

ISBN 978-1-59309-978-7
ISBN 978-1-50111-935-4 (ebook)
LCCN 2016948653

First Strebor Books trade paperback edition October 2016

Cover design: www.mariondesigns.com
Cover photograph: © Keith Saunders/Keith Saunders Photos

10 9 8 7 6 5 4 3 2 1

Manufactured in the United States of America

For information regarding special discounts for bulk purchases, please contact Simon & Schuster Special Sales at 1-866-506-1949

The Simon & Schuster Speakers Bureau can bring authors to your live event. For more information or to book an event, contact the Simon & Schuster Speakers Bureau at 1-866-248-3049 or visit our website at www.simonspeakers.com.

ACKNOWLEDGMENTS

First, let me thank the Almighty for the things he has done for me. To my ancestors who continue to direct my path even from the other side, thank you. Writing is a lonely passion, however, I feel surrounded by a wonderful village of people who truly believe in my work. To my agent, thank you, Sara. And, to Simon & Schuster and Strebor Books, thank you so much for choosing me. I would like to thank my girlfriends Twyla, Rhea, Ronnie, Kay, Betty, Waple, Andrea, Jennifer and Cheryl for your continuous love and support. And special thanks to my author friends, Stephanie Perry Moore, Janie Spataro, Barbara Bretton, Victoria Christopher Murray, and Zane. To Min. Jennifer D. Walton, Marva Greene, Atty. Karen Robinson-Ingram, Velma Larkins, Dionne Hall Huffman, Antionette Waits, C'celia Vernon and Margo Moorer for giving me that extra support. And, to the members of Delta Sigma Theta Sorority, Inc., I appreciate you for allowing me the opportunity to showcase my talent in our grand sisterhood. None of my success would be possible without the support of my fans, and the bookclubs. Last and most importantly, I'd like to thank my loving family for their support, which allows me the freedom to do what I love most—write books.

PROLOGUE

T he twin girls ambled side by side down the cobblestone sidewalk on Broad Street, their noses stuck in the air as if they were sniffing lilacs in the spring. But it was cold. The winter breeze lifted their coattails as they hurried to their destination. One of the girls swung her arms loosely as if she had to propel herself forward. They walked with a purpose, looking straight ahead. They trampled through the shadows of the pine trees lining the rocky city streets, and down the uneven cobblestone sidewalk, stepping in perfect unison. I stood across the street beside a bare tree, gazing at them as I braced myself against the cold air, shivering, even though the sun was high. No one appeared to pay them much attention; however, I couldn't keep my eyes off them, pinpointing their every move. A lady walking down the sidewalk spoke to them and both smiled and said hello at the same time. Afterward, their rosy cheeks lit up. They were dressed alike in red plaid coats with black cloches on their heads. From across the street, I studied them hard to see if I could tell them apart. They were easily five feet in height, but one of them appeared to be a slight bit taller.

I have developed this curious fascination with identical twins. Though rarely did I see siblings of the same birth. But, ever since Kindred Camm appeared in Richmond, wearing a camel Fedora tilted over his left eye, and dressed in brown cuffed trousers, the spitting image of no-good Herman Camm, my deceased step-father who had raped me, I find myself searching for a difference, intentionally studying the mannerisms and statures of twins. How else could you tell them apart? There is always some way to tell them apart, although it might be so minor, you have to hunt for it.

I reflected back to the summer when the State Fair came to Richmond, Virginia. Simon and I jumped at the thought of seeing clowns and the acrobats swinging high above the crowd doing tricks, leaving our mouths wide open. Everyone in Jackson Heights vowed to get to the fair. Inhaling the stench of sweaty horses and tiny monkeys, we ended up in a tent to view the famous freak show. Inside on a raised stage were the faces of the strangest twins I had ever seen, the Muse Brothers. They were an alabaster color, so white it hurt my eyes to look at them, and their eyelids were a ghostly pink. It was an eerie feeling. Even the pigeon paused his chirping at the mere sight of them. Their hair was curly like us colored folks, and they had our wide noses and full lips. Folks said they were albinos. So, as the white people gathered to get a closer look, pushing and pointing amid raucous giggling, my heart ached for the colored boys on display like Mandingo slaves. As the tears welled up in my eyes, I fought them back to keep Simon from seeing me cry. But when I saw the two women on display as the Monkey and Snake women, the tears trickled uncontrollably down my cheeks. One of them had scales for skin and the other wore a swimsuit which drew our eyes to the hair all over her body, like that of an animal. The highlight of the show was another set of twins. When the barker asked them to "rise," my chest heaved at the sight of them joined together at the hip. The twins didn't say anything as the anxious crowd sighed, whispered and even chuckled. The Siamese twins stood still, on display, as the carnival barker said, "The freak show is just beginning!

Come see how these girls are attached at the hip." It was a lousy display of humankind, and I found no entertainment in gazing at someone born with an imperfection. I remember overhearing someone calling them retarded. What a travesty!

Back in the present, just knowing Kindred, Herman's twin, was in town had me mystified. From the moment I'd laid eyes on him at the club, I'd been edgy. My heart raced at the sight of him. It was complete trepidation; he had me worried. And he was everywhere. Running into him at the corner store, my hands became clammy and beads of sweat trickled down my forehead and onto my nose. When he grinned at me, I balled up my fist like I had with Herman, ready to fight. I ran out of the store like a terrified child. He had even been spotted at church, a place Herman despised. The Fedora tilted to the side, covering his beady eye, and the starched suits with pressed pleats were all too similar to the man we were longing to forget.

Seeing *Miss Pearl Brown* written on the large sign in front of the club was something to brag about. I was enchanted with Pearl Brown. Even with the expansion of the club, which created more seats, there still was standing room only whenever she performed. I couldn't wait to visit the club and listen to her bold voice command the attention of everyone in the room. Ms. Pearl's big voice had folks whistling, and gathering in crowded cars to come across town and from as far away as Washington, D.C. just to hear her sing.

Maggie Walker, the most important woman in the community, even took a back seat to Pearl Brown. Ms. Walker was the richest colored woman around, but she would never be as popular as Ms. Pearl. Ms. Pearl had the white people lining up to get into a colored club. And the club became the "in" place to be. It really was something unusual to see white people standing toe to toe in line with coloreds to hear Pearl belt out the blues. Most coloreds looked in the opposite direction to avoid making eye contact with the white folks. Everyone had to be there! Pearl had finally gotten the attention of some white men from New York, who now had a hand in managing her career.

Richmond was a pleasant place to live. I loved the cobblestone sidewalks and the glow of the street lamps at night. Watching the cars instead of mules was also fascinating. It was better than home to me. I had even gotten used to Ms. Pearl, and I liked the way she treated me. She was certainly not the liar people claimed her to be. She was just a woman without boundaries, who'd given me advice and warned me about women who don't take care of themselves. I was going to take her advice. There was no way I was going to let Kindred hurt me or my son. This time around, I had something for the twin.

CHAPTER 1

On Monday, January 2, 1922, *Orphans of the Storm* was showing at the theater downtown. Everybody complained about the film Mr. Griffin, the producer, had done in the past—*The Birth of a Nation*. It was said the white man had written some disturbing things about us coloreds; and seemingly he didn't have a problem with mistreating us. In the colored newspaper, The National Association for the Advancement of Colored People (NAACP) warned us about supporting his new work. I wanted to see the new show, had heard he was tackling abuse, but I knew demoralizing coloreds for entertainment was wrong. So, I decided to stay away from the theater and his work. "You don't need to see his new movie. Even if folks claim he has changed, he still doesn't care about us coloreds. He should have thought about us when he made his first movie degrading us," Simon said. "Besides, who wants to always be seated in the balcony of the theater?" So, we went to the club instead.

You could see the big sign way before we made it to the street corner. It read, "Pearl Brown Tonight." Rumors traveled that the owner of Okeh Records was also in town looking for new colored talent for his record label. The company had already released a hit from Mamie Smith, and it was selling everywhere. Finally, coloreds were on the radio. Hearing a record on the gramophone by Pearl Brown, would make all of Jefferson County proud, and Jackson Heights too.

We stood in line over thirty minutes to get inside the club. It snaked around the corner past the place that sold hamburgers and chit'ling plates on Sundays. Standing in line with us were three professional-looking white men, and a strange-looking white couple. I couldn't believe they were waiting with the rest of us. The men seemed important though—quiet and conscientious. They appeared to not mind being with coloreds. In my mind, if they wanted to go straight into the club, no one would murmur a word.

There was no charge to get into the place, but it was expected that you'd purchase a drink and a sandwich. Fried chicken, pork chops and hamburgers were on the menu. Most often we would snack on the free peanuts already on the tables. Once Simon and I were inside the club, we rushed to get a seat close to the stage. We found two vacant seats at a table with Adam Murphy and his date. Simon asked, "Can we sit with you two, Adam?"

Adam looked around. "I guess so," he answered, without any enthusiasm.

"We will sit here, Carrie," said Simon, pulling out a chair next to Adam Murphy.

I frowned at the thought of sitting with Adam. I wasn't sure I would enjoy sharing him with the attractive, cocoa brown girl with shoulder-length hair leaning all over him. Before we sat at the table, she flashed a bleak smile. I smiled back even though I had no desire to get to know her.

"There are some vacant tables in the back," I whispered, trying to avoid what was about to happen.

"I thought you wanted to be up front," Simon retorted. I didn't comment.

Simon must have realized something was bothering me, "You all right?"

"Yes, we will have a good view from here of Ms. Pearl when she performs," I answered, knowing I had to concentrate to keep my almost former lover, Adam, out of my mind. His sexy eyes stared me as though we were the only ones at the table. I couldn't look him in the eyes.

Simon, seated across from Adam, asked, "What have you been up to, Man? I haven't seen you since you were at the house for dinner." Adam bit his lip before speaking to Simon. After all, Simon had threatened him, told him to stay away from me, and leave me alone. Now, he was acting like Adam was not a threat.

"I'm still in school," Adam replied.

"Where do you go to school?" Simon queried.

"I go here in Richmond."

"So being in Petersburg didn't work for you, huh?" Simon commented sarcastically.

"Naw," Adam answered, frowning.

Simon had been acting a bit uneasy. His dark eyes were darting around the room as if he were expecting someone to show up.

"Do you want something to drink, Baby?" he finally asked, getting up from the table.

"Water will be fine," I replied.

Simon stood up and took off toward the bar, his eyes casing the area looking as if he was unsure of something. He had been cautious ever since Willie was shot and murdered. "I'm not going to close my eyes and let something like that happen again," he'd said. All the women were paying attention to him. His broad athletic shoulders and beautiful white teeth caused even the white women to turn around and smile at him. One woman sitting near the bar threw her hand out as he passed the table where she was sitting. He reached back and tapped her hand to acknowledge her. It should have been a crime for a man to be that beautiful. As I was watching Simon, my mind wandered to Adam, who was sitting across from me. Adam's attractiveness was subtle. His inviting dark eyes and seriousness made him mysterious. Whatever Adam was whispering to his date caused her eyes to light up and a wide smile rippled across her face. I watched, and an envious frown creased my forehead. What was he saying? In the past, he had murmured in my ear that had I not been married, he would have had me permanently smiling.

It was frigid outside, and the air was moist like it might snow. However, no one would believe it by the number of people coming through the door of the club. The cold weather usually made people stay home, but not tonight. For a long time after Willie was shot, I was afraid to return to the club. I would dream about the night I crawled around on the floor as my heart pounded out of my chest, trying to avoid the gunshots that took Willie's life. It wasn't until the owner put a sign on the door and closed it down for remodeling, that I considered stepping foot back into the place. He expanded the seating area and repainted. It looked brand-new. With the changes, many people had forgotten the cruel way Willie had been murdered. He was shot down like a dog. Ms. Pearl witnessed it too. The air was new tonight, and I intended to enjoy the show no matter how much Adam Murphy stared at me.

Simon returned to the table with my glass of water and a dark drink for himself.

"Here you go," he said, handing me my water.

"Thank you," I responded as I looked around at all the people arriving, dressed in their finest.

Sensing Adam peering at me from across the table, I turned my head away to avoid locking eyes with him. Simon had his arm around my chair, and he pulled me close to him. Adam did the same thing to the woman sitting with him, and she appeared to enjoy it. Tonight was going to be interesting.

The white men who'd been in line with us, whom I now assumed were from the record company, sat right in the center of the room. Both of them sipped on dark drinks with ice while waiting for the famous Pearl Brown to perform. Moments earlier, I had seen Simon walk over to the table where they were sitting and shake their hands. The men smiled at Simon as if they knew him. But now we all sat anxiously waiting for Ms. Pearl to walk up to the stage. It was her custom always to be a few minutes late. I wasn't sure if it was something all performers did. When she strolled up to the stage wearing a tight-fitting, shimmery beige dress, hair curled under and falling on her shoulders, and bright-red lips, the crowd broke out into thunderous applause. Some people rose to their feet. I didn't, only shifted my eyes throughout the room. Adam and Simon stood clapping. She was certainly a star, and she knew it. She smiled at us, and waved. Before she began to sing, she addressed the crowd, "Thank you for the love. I really mean it."

"We love you!" was heard throughout the room.

Ms. Maggie Walker, the first colored banker, strutted through the door just as Pearl began to sing. She was the only person in the room with reserved seating. She was donned in a brown mink coat and, as usual, a man with a mustache was holding her arm. When she sat down, Pearl stopped singing just to greet her. "So glad to see you, Ms. Walker. Y'all, give our banker a hand." Ms. Walker smiled and acknowledged Pearl with a wave. Continuing to sing, Pearl gently moved into her rhythm; I felt chills travel throughout my body. She had that effect on me. I couldn't help noticing Adam and how he was kissing the girl he was with on the cheek. There was something about the way Pearl swayed and sang that made couples want to touch. I grabbed Simon's hand and a subtle smile released across his face. She sang three more songs before she came down from the stage. Music was like magic in my ears. Even though I enjoyed her sounds, Adam's attentiveness to his date rattled my nerves. I rolled my eyes and cringed at the sight of them.

After a while, Adam's presence did not bother me. Simon had made sure of that. He pulled me close into his big arms and made me feel as though I was the only one in the room. It was like when we'd first met. Feeling secure with him, I knew no one would be able to hurt me. Adam watched us intensely. He even tried to spark up a conversation with Simon. "Man, are you still playing ball?"

"Yeah, I will always be playing ball." After he answered, the conversation dwindled to nearly nothing. I felt it was a way to pull Simon away from me. I knew Adam was jealous.

After taking a fifteen-minute break, Ms. Pearl returned to the stage with even more vigor. I couldn't keep still, was swaying from left to right. Her voice was so rich. The white men seemed to gaze at her in awe. I knew after her final rendition, Okeh Records would rush to sign her up. Simon enjoyed the music too. But at times, he was standing near the bar as if he was hoping to run into someone. Adam and his date were quiet. They didn't seem to have much in common; she slid motionlessly into his arms staring straight ahead as if she was bored. I was certain it was just a date of convenience because he had been gawking at me all night. We stayed until Ms. Pearl sang her last song.

When the show was over, Simon came back to the table and assisted me with my coat. "You leaving?" Adam asked.

I turned to answer him, but Simon answered first. "The show is over."

Adam grinned. Then he helped his date with her coat.

It was strange leaving at the same time as Adam and his date. As we followed the crowd exiting the club, I sensed something strange. I looked over my shoulder and in the corner was Herman Camm's twin staring straight at me with a wide smile on his face. It scared me, so I pointed him out to Simon.

"That man is not paying you any attention, Carrie."

"He is, I promise you," I said, attempting to convince him. Instead, he shook his head in disbelief.

Adam was behind us and overheard me trying to convince Simon of Herman's presence. He reached down and touched my hand without Simon ever noticing. Then he said to Simon, "Man, that cat *was* smiling at Carrie."

Simon didn't say a word. He grabbed my hand and pulled me through the door and down the cobblestone sidewalk. I turned around and Adam was standing with his date, watching us scurry down the street.

CHAPTER 2

Late one evening as we were settling down, Simon announced he was leaving to play ball. It was in the heart of winter. I peered out the window at the dull sky and snow flurries, the moon hidden behind the clouds leaving an anvil silhouette for the imagination. Thoughts were bouncing around in my head. Where on earth does anyone play ball in this weather? I opened the front door, stuck my head out and sniffed the moist scent of snow in the air. At first the snowflakes began to fall and melt on the ground, and now a blanket of snow was covering the street and tree limbs. Simon assured me he was headed down south where the weather was mild, and they played baseball all year round.

"We are heading to New Orleans to train with the colored boys down there. Folks around here say they are good baseball players. Some people think them boys are better than we are," Simon said, sitting on the bed vigorously stuffing clothes into his duffle bag.

I wanted to believe him. He loved baseball and lived it every day of his life. I had to listen to stories about how Pete Hill had hit more home runs than any white baseball player. He said Pete, a leftie, often tricked his opponents by hitting with either hand. A baseball powerhouse is what they said about him. Simon also talked about Rube Foster and how he was making it right for coloreds. He said the National Negro League was taking off and the white baseball players were finally respecting the colored talent. Besides, Rube Foster was the best player ever. When he talked about it, his eyes lit up and a smile would fill his face from ear to ear. He loved the game of baseball and didn't mind talking about it to anyone who would listen But Ms. Pearl, and Nadine, my chocolate and beautiful neighbor overly fascinated with Simon, said they had seen him when I thought he was out of town.

I stood watching him pack, moving with him around the bedroom. "People say you are in town when you say you are out of town playing ball."

He stopped stuffing clothes in the bag and stood straight up and shook his head. "Carrie, ain't no way they saw me. I was out of town with the team. I just don't understand why people will make up lies. You know they are jealous of us." He stuffed a pair of trousers into the duffle bag. Nadine might be jealous with a childish crush on my husband, but there was no way Ms. Pearl, with all her fame, was jealous of me. She was living her dream as a singer, and everybody knew her. They even said she was better than Bessie Smith. There was no reason to be jealous of us.

I shook my head. "I just don't see people mistaking you for somebody else, Simon. You stand out in a crowd."

"I'm not the only tall man around, you know!" he argued, agitated by the inferences.

"You are right about that," I agreed. However, Simon was tall and muscular and with one glimpse, people knew he was an athlete. He had absolutely no fat on his body, just lean muscle. He stood out amongst most of the puny men in the community. He was the only athlete anybody talked about in Jackson Heights, where we lived. And most everybody knew him.

"There is a cat that comes to the club, people think looks exactly like me. But I don't think so."

I smacked my lips, and sat down. "Do you remember the time when I came home early and Nadine was sitting at my kitchen table?" He nodded his head yes. "You were supposed to be out of town then too." He glanced over at me, swallowed and took a step backward. I knew I had struck a raw nerve then. His mood changed. The frowns were lining up across his forehead.

He raised his voice and attempted to explain. "I had just got in! Nadine saw me put the key in the door and ran across the street. I didn't know what she wanted! Something is wrong with that woman, I tell you!" All the while he was talking, I noticed the frowns increasing on his face, and the way he forcibly stuffed clothes in the bag. He was upset!

I was determined to get an answer along with a reaction. "Simon, please don't lie to me," I pleaded. "We have been honest all this time. Now is not a good time to start lying."

I could tell he was unsettled, although now he was forcing a smile. Simon slid over on the bed and put his arm around my shoulder. "I am not lying to you, girl. I love you. Now stop listening to everything people around here say. These folk don't want to see you happy."

I softened, and believed him. He had been there for me ever since the first time I'd met him in Jefferson County. I remembered how my heart fluttered at the sight of him. He was a gentleman and very patient with me. The times when we were alone and snuggled in each other's arms, he could have convinced me to give in to the passion; instead he was patient. He'd taken care of me in many ways, and accepted my bastard son as if he was his own. There was no reason to doubt him now. Besides, Nadine would definitely lie. She was no more than the neighborhood tramp to me, who couldn't keep her eyes off my handsome husband. I remembered how she'd questioned me the first week I was in town. She had come over to my house for a cup of sugar, and instead had questions for me. "Why did you come to Richmond? It is not like the country," she'd said. I had gazed her directly in her eyes and answered, "I came to be with my husband." She'd tooted her lips up, glanced at my husband, stared directly at him, and allowed lust to overtake her. She was trying my patience.

I watched Simon tuck his dress trousers into the duffle bag with a matching shirt, and then he glanced around at me. He added underpants, long johns, and more than enough clothes to last for several weeks. Outside, snow clouds were hanging low in the gray sky, and the wind was twirling around the few leaves left shivering on the barren trees. And he was going to play baseball in the wintertime…

It wouldn't be long before I, too, would be leaving for school. I had enjoyed the sabbatical away from Petersburg, which was almost as boring as Jefferson County. The time away had given me an opportunity to bond with my son who was precariously walking around and picking up things only a fine eye could see. Little Robert watched his daddy fill up the duffle bag. At times he pulled on Simon's trousers to get his attention. "I'll be back, little man," he told him, patting him on the head. He smiled and reached for Simon who was folding a long-sleeved shirt and stuffing it in the bag. *If it is so mild, then why is he carrying so many winter clothes with him?* I wondered.

Once he was done, he picked up Robert and sat him on his lap. "I am going to take Robert downstairs to Mrs. Hall's house. She's been asking about him."

He wrapped Robert in a heavy blanket. Down the steps they went to Mrs. Hall's with Robert balanced on his shoulders, and Robert smiling all the way. Robert loved it when he carried him that way, and would often fake a cry when Simon put him down.

I went into the bathroom to freshen up. I searched under the basin for my sponge and soaked it in a few drops of vinegar and water. I had to be careful not to use too much vinegar since it would burn my skin. I wrung out the excess water and inserted the sponge deep inside of me.

Simon came back up the steps singing. Across the street in the dark, Nadine was on the porch and waving while the wind was blowing her hair astray. She was a pathetic excuse for a mother, I thought. She did anything to get the attention of a man, especially Simon. If it meant catching a cold from being in the wintery weather, it didn't matter. Simon waved at her and yelled, "You had better go inside; it is cold out here."

"I know," she hollered back. "I just wanted to speak to you. I haven't seen you in a while." She stood with her hands on her hips, while the wind lifted her dress above her knees.

"I am on the way back out," Simon yelled back at her.

"Be safe, and hurry back," she said, flipping her hair out of her face. "Take care of yourself. When will you be back?"

"I'm not sure," he said and came into the house. I glanced out of the window and Nadine was still standing outside, the wind blowing her dress and her curls, the snow flurries sticking onto the porch. Her balusters were already snow covered.

Simon quickly sealed up his bag. Leaning it against the door, he pulled me by the hand and led me into the bedroom. He gazed into my eyes, and then started to undress himself. He quickly removed his shirt, showing the hairs on his muscular chest. He unbuttoned his trousers and they fell to the floor. I knew what to expect. He removed my blouse and exposed my heavy breasts. Afterward, he took off my skirt and panties; they toppled to the floor. Flames from the fireplace lit up the room. The coal furnace was a great source of heat, but it was cozy watching the sparks from the burning wood dance in the air. With the lights off, it was a beautiful sight. Instead of getting into bed, we decided to lie in front of the fireplace, on top of a quilt Momma had made. He started caressing me. My body twitched, and all of a sudden, I was hot all over. He kissed me and pushed the bulge in his shorts against me. When he began to kiss my neck, I could feel the warmth take over my limbs, and the sweat pop out of my skin. At the moment his tongue traveled down from my collar bone to my stomach, I was squirming. I ran my hands up his back and massaged his shoulders as his tongue explored my body. When he turned me over to enter me, I thought about the sponge I had inserted. I didn't ever want him to know I used it. When our bodies connected, I moaned like it was my first time. Oh what a night!

I was completely still. My breath stabilized as I watched him go into the bathroom and return with a wash towel. When he gave it to me, I smiled and stretched out on the quilt butt naked. After cuddling bare for a while, I decided to put on one of my house dresses.

"You gon' be all right?" Simon asked, buttoning up his shirt.

"I'm fine." I picked up my clothes from the floor on the way to the bathroom. I dislodged the sponge, washed it, wrapped it in a wash cloth and stuffed it way back in the corner of the pine cabinet underneath the sink. I returned to the bedroom where Simon was sitting on the bed, and flopped down beside him. I hesitated before asking one last time, "Why are you leaving in the heart of the winter? Baseball is played in the spring and summer."

Simon answered quickly, without even looking at me. "We are going down south to play because it is warm there. It is damn near sixty-five degrees at night folks say." I noticed he'd packed more winter things than warm weather clothing.

"It just doesn't sound right. Nobody leaves their family in the winter."

Simon was shaking his head back and forth, and then he exploded, "Woman, why can't you get this in your head? I love baseball!"

"You don't need to get loud," I said. "It just doesn't make sense to be playing out somewhere in the cold weather when your family is home in the warmth. Do you see the snow falling out there?" I pointed out.

The frowns in his forehead disappeared. "Remember I will be back in a few weeks. Meanwhile, go to school and concentrate on your schoolwork. Before you know it, I will be opening the front door."

There was something about our conversation that didn't feel right. A cold chill traveled throughout my body. Either it was my nerves or my intuition telling me he was lying again. Nobody with any sense would be traveling down south or anywhere in the snow. Even down south the men took a break in the wintertime.

It was cold, snowy, and pitch-black when Simon got into his car. I waved at him from the front door and threw him a kiss, not knowing where he might lay his head.

CHAPTER 3

My momma stepped through the door two days after Simon left. She came wagging an oversized leather suitcase packed full to capacity with enough clothes to last more than a month. It was as if she already knew Simon was on the road, or had seen him somewhere. She was all wrapped up and shielded from the wind. She had a red scarf she had knitted wrapped tight round her neck, a man's hat on her head, and thick stockings tied in a knot above the knee. She had on the old folks' comforts she had ordered from New York that came above her ankles, almost like boots. She was country for sure, and everyone could tell. She knocked on the door, and when I cracked it open, she was standing on the porch kicking the snow off her shoes. Coming inside, she set her suitcase down on the floor and slid it into the corner of the kitchen. She stood up, stretched her back, took off her coat and scarf and handed them to me. I hung them up on the coat rack and proceeded to pour her a cup of coffee, which had been keeping warm on the stove. "Not too much," she said, demonstrating with her hand the amount. Before she took a sip, she searched the kitchen with her eyes as if she was expecting someone else to be there. I really didn't know what caused her to do that, but shortly afterward, while sipping her coffee and watching the smoke billow in the air, she paused as if she had a sudden thought. She peered straight into my eyes with a serious stare, which made me a little uncomfortable.

"I'm here to help you, Chile. I know how hard it is to manage without a man 'round to do things for you. Ever since my husband died, I've had to do all the thinking around the house." I wondered if she was spooked or something. She acted as if she knew something bad and I desperately needed her help.

I smacked my lips and before she noticed, I smiled. "I think I manage okay when Simon's gone, Momma...ain't that right, Robert?" Robert looked up at me with his beady little eyes and grinned. The two teeth he had in his mouth gleamed like shiny pearls.

"Whether you admit it or not, you need help," she said. "No woman needs to be living in a city like this without her husband. Do you even know these people around here?" I hesitated to answer her because I really loved being in my neighborhood and around the people. It was a colorful community, and everybody spoke and welcomed you. There was a beauty salon around the corner, a butcher down the street, a school a block over, and a church or two within walking distance. It was a fully serviced community. And, it was the place I had envisioned when I was in Jefferson County.

I shook my head no. "I know my neighbors. Everybody around here seems to be real nice."

"Does that woman still live over yonder?" Momma said, nodding her head toward Nadine's house.

"Are you talking about Nadine?" I asked, only to agitate her more. I could tell our conversation was turning sour. Nadine was not someone I wanted to think about.

"That floozie who is always chasing after yo' husband... you know who I'm talking about," she said matter-of-factly with her head tilted to the side waiting for me to comment.

"She is still across the street," I replied.

"You know you need to watch her. She is one who no woman should trust. She is just like Pearl Brown."

"Momma, you are so different these days," I said, listening to her blurt out these things.

"What on earth are you talking about?"

"You used to be quiet. Now you are saying things about people you would have slapped me in the mouth for mentioning."

"Well, it is the truth. I haven't said anything I am ashamed of yet, Chile," she commented, with a sly yet serious grin on her face.

"Momma, I don't really want to talk about Nadine. She's just a neighbor and not a friend. I'm not worried about her, and further-more, I don't know much about her."

"You should worry, Chile, and keep yo' eyes wide open too. That woman is dangerous, I tell ya. I would make it my business to get to know her."

I struggled to keep quiet so I bit my bottom lip and just listened to Momma talk, even though I had something I really wanted to say. I got up from the table, and inhaled to get my nerve up. "Momma, you just got here. Isn't there something else to talk about other than Nadine? How is everybody doing in Jefferson?" I said, changing the subject.

Momma sucked her lips and released a sigh. She cleared her throat, and then asked me to sit back down. She turned toward me and gazed straight into my eyes. It was an intimidating stare, so I looked away. "I am old enough to say whatever I want to. I never raised you to be disrespectful, and I ain't taking it now. I was just giving you a bit of wisdom. You should listen and keep any sassing to yo'self. You know better. Don't you let being up here in the city make you no fool, Chile." Her words sucked away my courage.

I quickly got in line. I had said way too much and knew it. "I'm sorry, Momma," I apologized.

Momma didn't say anything. Instead, she shook her head. "I am going in the back room, unpack and put my grandson down for a nap."

She got up from the table, picked up her suitcase along with Robert who had been reaching for her and whining all along, and shuffled into the bedroom.

Mrs. Hall had Robert spoiled. She had been baking cookies especially for him, and allowing him to have his way. I didn't hesitate to spank his hands when he touched something he shouldn't have. Having Momma with us would give Mrs. Hall, who babysat when I was away at school, a break from Robert. Although Robert enjoyed being with her, she would forget to discipline him. Now he was accustomed to whining in an attempt to get his way.

Momma loved taking care of Robert. For once in my life, I saw her with my own eyes showing affection to him. She had never been one to kiss on her children, and she never returned Papa's nurturing hugs and kisses. But, the first thing she did when she came in the door was to reach down and kiss Robert on his round cheeks. When she did, a smile rippled across his face. I always wanted her to show some kind of affection to me and my brothers, but instead, she was no-nonsense and straight to the point. It was like she resisted the intimacy that came along with being a mother. I resented her for being so unapproachable.

Momma puzzled me when she informed me Simon was gone. *Did some kind of bird fly and whisper it in her ear?* It had to be the reason she had come unannounced on the train and carrying with her enough clothes to stay awhile. My aunt Ginny was noted for premonitions and forecasting the future and some folk believed she was some sort of witch. Now, Momma had me wondering the same things about her.

Momma caught me staring mindlessly out of the kitchen window when she returned from the bedroom swinging her arms as if she was now in control. She finally had some people to watch over. I found myself gazing at the snow flurries sticking on Nadine's porch, and my eyes were roaming up and down the street in hopeless anticipation, wishing Simon had decided to return home.

"Why is your face so sad, Chile?" Momma asked.

"I'm not sad, Momma. I was just thinking."

Her eyes grew concerned. "What are you worried about? You got Simon on your mind, Chile. I can tell."

"Momma, how did you know Simon was gone?" I asked, waiting for one of those answers only soothsayers or root workers could come up with.

Instead, she paused before answering me. "Well, I ran into 'im the other day at the feed store. He told me he was heading south to play baseball, and had stopped off in Jefferson County to see a friend."

Her response was a relief for me. Now I could breathe. "Did you believe him?"

"I don't know. You can't put nothing past nobody these days. Folks done seen him with them white men in town, though."

"What men, Momma?"

"Chile, you need to listen to yo' own instincts," she said, ignoring my original question. Then she continued, "I don't pay too much attention to the peoples around. They always got something to say, but experience tells me there is some truth in parts."

"Momma, you never answered me. "

"Well, your brother Carl seen him with one of them white men who makes liquor up in the woods. But that don't mean nothing. I advise you to trust yo' own gut," she answered, patting her chest. "If you feel something is wrong, it probably is," she added, staring out the window watching Nadine's children throw snow-balls at each other.

"Did you think Herman was going to turn out like he did?" I asked.

Immediately, her eyes became slits, her expression changed and a frown washed across her forehead so fast, I sealed my lips. I became a bit fidgety myself, and started to shake my leg. It was the first time I had attempted to get her to open up about her former husband, Herman Camm. It seemed minutes passed by before a word was said, and it appeared as if each tick on the wall clock became louder and more profound as I waited for her to respond.

She finally broke the silence in the room. "I had to think for a minute." I waited for her to continue, but it was silent again. Then she cleared her throat." I believe I knew about Herman, but I wanted to believe the best about 'im. You see everybody needs a chance."

"Did you know about me, Momma?" I gently asked. I wondered if she knew that Herman had raped me.

She locked her hands across her chest and twirled her thumbs. "No, I didn't know. I didn't 'spect none of that to happen. I just knew he drinked way too much liquor, and liquor makes peoples act a fool. I did know 'bout Pearl Brown. She had a thing for 'im. I never thought about you, Chile. People can certainly fool you."

"Momma," I said, relishing the conversation, knowing she had always been so tight-lipped, and secretive. Now she was commu-nicating like the mother I had longed for growing up in Jefferson County. I could not forget watching my best friend Hester's mother talking and laughing with her. I had wanted the same with my mother, but she couldn't do it. It hurt me. Now, this was special since I'd always yearned for her to share things with me. Yet, she was still making excuses for Herman.

"I had no idea Simon was stopping over in Jefferson County. He said he was headed down south."

"Sometimes men go off and don't say a word. Your daddy went off one time and stayed most of the day and all night. I didn't know where the man was. I sent your brother looking for him. He came back with nothing. I come to find out, he was over at his momma's, hiding. He said he needed to get away from me to think. Now, nobody would believe he run off, but he did. He was not a perfect man."

Listening to her open up was like music to my ears. It didn't matter what the subject, this was a beginning. No matter what she said, nothing could explain my husband playing baseball in the heart of the winter. Being in Jefferson County was something else I couldn't understand. Why was he around those corrupt white men? By now, he should have been in New Orleans.

Momma shook her head. "Carrie, don't spend too much time trying to figure it all out. We women have other things to worry about... Robert go' be getting up in a minute, and we got some cooking to do."

I chuckled. "You are right."

I walked over to the pantry and gathered several Irish potatoes from the vegetable bin. Got a knife and I handed them to Momma, and she began to peel potatoes. I couldn't wait to taste her potato soup with ham and onions. It was perfect for the cold, snowy weather.

CHAPTER 4

I tapped hard on the door and stood waiting, shivering. Even though the sun shone bright and my shadow was cast on the ground, the strong winds braised my cheeks like sandpaper and they were rosy as if I had applied rouge. I knocked even harder when no one came to the door. Just when I had turned to leave, my knuckles white from knocking as hard as I could, the door cracked open. Adam peeked around the door seal. "Where are you going?"

"It's cold out here. I was about to leave." I smiled, pulling the collar of my coat close up around my neck.

Adam grinned. "Come on in." And he opened the door wide, revealing the beautiful mahogany pillars in the foyer of the antebellum tenement house. Adam was the first person I'd met in Richmond. He was somewhat responsible for me finding a school to attend. He had become my mentor and friend, and convinced me it was all right to go to school with a child. He was the most progressive colored man I had ever met. Many believed a woman's place was barefoot, pregnant and in the kitchen. We had so much in common. He was young, ambitious, and had dreams similar to mine. I really enjoyed being around him. As usual, Adam was dressed well. He had on a white shirt with a brown bow tie. His hair was neatly cut and there was no hair visible on his chocolate skin. He was what the old women called well trained, and simply refined. He had all the makings of a perfect gentleman.

Inside, I immediately felt the warmth from the fire burning in his sitting room. I went straight to the fireplace and rubbed my hands together until they began to warm up. The heat felt good after forging through the wind. Adam lived upstairs, along with three other tenants who rented rooms. We took a seat on a Victorian davenport with a red-and-tan paisley design. It was a bit airy because of the high ceilings, so, I slid over closer to the fireplace.

"To what do I owe this visit?" Adam asked as he helped me take off my coat and hat. He threw them over the high-back chair. The enormous room felt empty, since it had only two chairs, a table and a davenport, and a book shelf filled with works by W. E. B. Dubois, Booker T. Washington and Josephine Brown. On the wall was a large mirror which faced the window, and in the mirror was the reflection of the street and everything happening outside. I slid closer to Adam to warm up and we sat perfectly still for a few minutes without uttering a word. Occasionally, I'd glance at the mirror to admire the Model T cars going up the street alongside the horse and buggies.

"Why are you here, Carrie?" he asked me in a serious tone, minus the usual smile.

"I just wanted to visit. I wanted to catch up on everything, find out about school," I said even though the truth was that I missed him and longed to see him. He had a crazy effect on me, something hard to explain.

He shook his head as if he was baffled by my response. "I don't want any trouble with Simon. He warned me about being in the company of his wife. And we have a gentleman's agreement. I promised to leave his wife alone."

"How did you feel about that?" I asked and paused for him to gather his thoughts.

"I don't know how I feel. Am I supposed to be angry with him, or with you?"

"Shouldn't you just ignore him, because we are friends?"

He glanced over at me and stared. "Is that what you wanted me to do? I thought you wanted to be with your husband."

I thought about what he said. Why was I there and not home with my child and mother who needed me? I told Momma I was going downtown to purchase a garter and hosiery to wear to school. But a compelling detour to see Adam altered my plan. I wanted to be with Simon; however, something inside me was missing Adam. I questioned myself about it and really didn't have an answer. I walked right past the Miller and Rhodes store without even looking at the mannequin with the latest fashions in the window.

"I love my family, Adam, but you are my friend. Believe it or not, you are the first person I met when I moved to Richmond."

"You are avoiding answering my question. Why are you really here?"

I struggled with the words, my mouth dry and numb. "I wanted to see you," I finally blurted, mumbling the words as if I was embarrassed for what I had said.

"But why?" he asked, first standing and then pacing across the hardwood floor, which resonated the clunking sound of his heels with each step.

"I'm not sure why. All I can say is I wanted to see you."

He turned around and gazed in my eyes. The seriousness in his eyes reminded me of his no-nonsense yet caring character—how he had helped me understand what colleges were available for me in the city, and how he had traveled with me to visit the schools. He attended Virginia Union University, since it was the place most of the Baptist preachers got their education in theology.

Now he was asking me a question I didn't have the courage to answer. I was a married woman.

So I changed the subject. "Where is your friend?"

"What friend?"

"The girl from the club…"

"She's not around."

"Is she your girlfriend?"

He sat back down. "I don't understand why you are asking about her. You won't tell me the truth about why you are here."

I sighed. "I wanted to see you. You are the only real friend I have around here."

"I'll answer for you. Simon is out of town and you are feeling alone again. I'm your second thought."

"No, that is not true. Well, Simon is out of town, but you are not my second thought. I think about you all the time. "

A subtle smile spread across Adam's face. He reached over and grabbed my hand. "I think about you too. I just wanted to hear you admit it." I grinned thinking he wanted to see me too.

We both sat there in the big airy room hand in hand, watching the kindling sparks, relishing the moment, and neither of us mumbled a word. After a few minutes of total silence, I finally informed Adam I was going back to school, and I'd be leaving in a few days.

"You should go. Your son will not remember you being gone. He is too young. I'm proud of you," he said, smiling.

"I feel so guilty, though."

"You have to get an education. It is a sure way to pay for your future, and to take care of your son. Teachers make a decent wage, and it is an honorable job."

"There is no way I was going to work in the field like my papa did all of his life. And Momma goes to Mrs. Ferguson's and does the work she doesn't want to do."

"You won't have to," he said. "But remember there aren't many jobs for coloreds, so we have to take advantage of every opportunity. An honest job with fair wages is all we want."

Adam had been going to school a little longer than I had. Ministering to coloreds was first and foremost on his mind. He'd confessed to being tired of seeing colored folks sit quietly and let the white man tell them how to live. He'd said to me, "It is time for us to have a pastor who will give the word of God and to advise on the choices we make." He was determined to get the most out of school and I was sure he would be successful. I loved the advice he'd given me. My brother John had gone away to college, and I admired him as well. Adam shared the same values as I did. We both wanted more in life than what had been promised to us coloreds, and would sacrifice anything to make it happen. I was leaving my son with the Hall family, and I didn't feel bad about it. I just didn't want my son to forget me.

We were happy just being in each other's company, without saying a word. It was so strange how he had that effect on me. The sounds of wood popping in the fireplace were more than enough. Every once in a while, I'd glance at him and catch him staring at me. We both giggled.

Adam and I enjoyed each other's company so much, we didn't need to talk. We could sit for hours and be happy without saying a word. It was like he understood me. So we sat there smiling like couples do after making love. It was a heartwarming experience, and for a moment, I forgot about being married to Simon. When I stood up to leave, Adam quietly stood also. He got his coat off the coat rack.

"I'm going with you," he said. "I'm going to make sure you get home safely."

I grinned. "I've got to stop by the department store before I go home."

"I know," he answered, helping me with my coat. "I'm going with you." When he began to help me with my coat, something happened. The gentleness of his touch excited me. I fought back the feeling to wrap my arms around his waist, and even kiss him on the lips. Instead, I turned and walked toward the door. He followed close behind me.

Miller and Rhoads was a good place to shop, but coloreds had to enter through a side door on Fifth Street. It sold some of the best clothes in town. I hated that I could not try on the clothes like the other women shopping, and it was simply because coloreds were not allowed in the dressing rooms. We had to take the clothes home without knowing if they were a perfect fit. I made most of my clothes anyway. I would have shopped at the Emporium, which was owned by Ms. Maggie Walker, but it was going out of business, and they didn't have much merchandise left to choose from. The white merchants had seen to that. Simon said, "Them crackers never wanted us to have anything. They were mean and didn't like us being anything but servants to them." I remembered how Mrs. Ferguson treated my momma, and it was one of the reasons I longed to get an education.

Adam and I walked across the street and several long blocks down to Broad Street. We entered the store on the side street. A white lady walked in with us and nearly knocked me down rushing to go through the door first. I had to take a deep breath to keep from grabbing the lady by her hair. We browsed through the store, amazed at everything on display. The white patrons turned up their noses and looked down on us. We ignored them. I purchased two pairs of silk stockings. The sales lady with premature wrinkles around her eyes, and brown freckles all over her face asked me to lay my money on the counter. I did what she asked and she handed my hose to me in a brown paper sack.

"She is rude," Adam whispered in my ear as we walked away.

"I know. I'm used to it," I murmured back to him.

"But we shouldn't be. We probably have more education than she does."

Before exiting the department store, which, aside from all the rudeness, was a fascinating place, I checked out the ladies' dresses, because I usually could make a dress just as nice. White folks didn't have anything on me. When we approached the door, I walked right into Kindred Camm, who was coming through the door. I flinched, felt my heart flutter, but kept moving.

"Good afternoon," he said, his beady eyes peering at me without even blinking.

I didn't say anything. I just sped up and so did Adam. When Adam looked back, he was out of sight.

My chest started to heave and I couldn't catch my breath. "Hold up," Adam said, grabbing me by the arm. "What is wrong with you?"

I slowed down after we reached the corner. "It is him. The man I told you about."

"Calm down; he didn't do anything but speak."

"He looks exactly like my stepfather. He is supposed to be his long-lost brother, but he is the spitting image of that evil man."

Adam put his arm around me. "I can tell he scares you. I'm not going to let him or anybody else hurt you, so don't worry."

As we walked down the street past the Jefferson Hotel with the tall white columns, I told him why I feared the man we saw in the store. He listened intently and then he asked, "Does Simon know how you feel?"

"Yes," I told him. "He thinks I am making too much of it. He said I need to get over it all. But it is hard to ignore someone who exactly resembles the man who hurt you."

Adam listened and kept his arm around me as if to offer protection. It was a good feeling.

"I see him at the club sometimes. I'm going to keep my eyes out for him. I believe you and I don't like how he makes you feel."

"That man is a constant reminder of my life in Jefferson County. I wish I didn't fear him so much."

"You have your reasons. Everybody has something or someone they fear, but you can't let him know he is making you feel that way. You've got to be strong."

"I know. I think he is Herman Camm. That man is not dead; he is still lurking around, trying to get my attention."

"You need to make sure Simon knows how you feel. You've got to tell him the man scares the hell out of you."

"He knows."

"Why in hell did he go down south knowing you fear this man so much?"

I didn't know how to explain it all. I hated Simon being gone, but maybe it was better having Adam around to make sure Robert and I were all right. Simon seemed to care only about baseball.

"He loves baseball, Adam." I found myself defending Simon.

As we turned the corner down through the neighborhood past Jackson Heights' famous club where Ms. Pearl performed, I desired to peek in to make sure Simon was really away on baseball business. My nerves settled after we had walked several blocks. The thought of Simon being away and Herman lurking around town was disturbing. Adam told me he would handle it.

"I'm going to keep an eye out for you. I'll be riding down to Petersburg with you too. I want to make sure this man is not following you. If he is, I will have to speak to him about it," he confidently said.

All the while he was speaking, I could see the concern in his dark eyes. Even though I was scared, I knew I would never let another man take advantage of me, especially now.

CHAPTER 5

Adam carried the weathered brown leather suitcase I'd borrowed from Aunt Ginny with pride to the train depot. He walked with his chest out and shoulders squared. I noticed some of the younger ladies whispering as we approached the depot. Ginny's suitcase had come in handy, especially since it contained enough clothes to last me for several weeks. Packed were a black and brown skirt, along with a wool cardigan and a few blouses. I had learned from my roommates in the boardinghouse how to mix and match clothes, and add accessories, so I wouldn't look the same each day. My wardrobe was minimal, but what I did own was in good condition. I held my head up high, just like Maggie Walker, our banker, did the first time I had seen her at the club. She had exemplified power, and I wanted to emulate her. Besides, Adam made me feel special. He was doing all of the things I had hoped Simon would do for me.

We stood waiting for the train to come, the brisk wind blowing my hair. I pulled my scarf up around my ears. Adam had a wool scarf waving in the wind around his neck. Two young ladies, around my age, maybe older, were waiting along with two older women I'd seen before. They were huddled together trying to keep warm. One of them was a regular on the train, and it appeared we were on the same schedule. The train came around the corner whistling, emitting steam from its chimney long before it came to a screeching halt. The sound alerted the six of us standing and waiting. The two older ladies immediately picked up their suitcases and formed a line. Adam and I gazed at each other and a grin spread across my face. It was time to go back to school and finish my education, and Adam was going all the way to Petersburg with me.

Nadine's old man, a porter, was the first one off the train. He let down the steps and an elderly colored man and woman stepped off the train. Nadine's man assisted them with their luggage and afterward, he walked over to me. "Carrie, let me get your bag for you," he said, staring at Adam.

"I've got her bag," Adam said, reaching down to pick it up.

"No problem, Sir; I'm just doing my job." Nadine's husband cut his eyes at Adam as if he had wronged him in some way. He walked back over toward the two women and took their suitcases out of their hands. One of them grabbed his arm and he escorted her up the steps along with the suitcases into the colored section of the train. He came back down the steps and stood. When Adam and I started up the stairs, he asked me, "Where's your husband?"

I looked back at him and answered, "He is not here."

"I hope you know what you are doing," he commented, as if warning me.

I didn't respond. However, Adam boldly said to him, "Man, mind your own business. She is not your wife."

A grimace overtook his smile. "I was not talking to you."

Adam threw up his hands. "Carrie, you all right?"

"Yes, I'm fine, Adam."

We found a seat in the front of the colored car. Adam insisted on me sitting on the inside, which was how we had walked down the street. As the train jolted and screeched, pulling out of the depot and looping around the curve, we noticed a circle of men standing in front of the corner store. As the train got closer, we recognized Kindred Camm standing in the midst of the men. He glanced up at the train, but kept on talking. I couldn't tell if he had seen me or not.

"There he is again," I said, pointing in his direction.

Adam put his arm around me. "He didn't see you, and he is not going to mess with you anyway. I am with you."

"You are not going to be in Petersburg forever."

"No, but I plan on making frequent trips to visit you. I will be watching that cat, making sure he does not get in your way."

I smiled and let my head relax in his arms. I felt secure and maybe too comfortable, knowing he was not my husband. As the train rambled through the woods, I wondered where my husband was. Was he really in New Orleans or was he somewhere watching me?

It wasn't long before the train was slowing down to a stop. Nadine's husband waved at me as we exited the train. I threw my hand up too. Adam and I began our trek side by side down the sidewalk to the rooming house. He took my luggage up the stairs and came back down and took a seat on the davenport in front of the fireplace. The kindling was sizzling as it burned, and the room was cozy and warm. There was another couple in the room along with Miriam, my roommate, who was reading a book. Adam didn't stay long, and we barely talked. We held hands inhaling the scent of burning wood, as the fire popped. About twenty minutes later, he got up to leave.

We stood in the doorway gazing into each other's eyes. Adam didn't say anything; he pulled me in close. My heart sped up. He kissed me on the lips, and it was sweet, like chocolate icing. One of the girls from the house had her eyes fixated on me and Adam the entire time. I stood in the doorway and watched Adam walk down the sidewalk through the pine trees until he was out of sight. I closed the door. When I turned around, Miriam was standing with her arms folded, shaking her head.

"What's wrong?" I asked her.

"Aren't you married?" she asked, as if she was my mother.

"I won't discuss that with you."

"I had hoped to get to know him better myself, and now you are taking up with him," she said, surprising me.

"He is just a friend."

"Since when do friends kiss on the lips? And, it was a passionate kiss."

I walked away and headed toward the stairs. "I've got to unpack."

"Wait, I need to talk to you." Miriam signaled for me to come back. "What is it?" I asked.

"I was just wondering. Is something going wrong between you and your husband?"

I was shocked at her intrusion. "We are fine."

"Does he know about Adam?"

"Adam is a friend, and it is none of your business," I said, inhaling to calm myself. She was offending me, and I was about to say some *choice words* to her.

She chuckled. "I guess I said the wrong thing to you."

She was reading my mind. "Miriam, I think what is happening in my life is not anybody's business."

"I thought after what happened last year, we had established ourselves as friends."

"We are friends. I just don't want to discuss Adam with you right now. You are asking personal questions and making me uncomfortable."

"Is it because you don't trust me?" We both stopped talking when two girls came in the door and went upstairs.

Once they were up the stairs, I continued, "No, not at all, Miriam. I am not feeling up to such questions tonight. Remember, I am just getting back, and need to unpack and relax before we start classes in the morning. I promise we can talk about it all later."

"Good. I'm glad you said that, because I could have sworn I saw Simon hanging around last night."

"Simon, you say?" All of a sudden, I wanted to hear more.

"Well, it looked like him," she said, letting her eyes roll back in her head as if she was thinking.

"Where did you see him? Was he here at the boardinghouse?"

"I thought I saw him drive off last night when I arrived. Maybe it was someone who looked like him. I am not really sure. Whoever it was drove the same kind of car he has."

My nerves began to unravel. I inhaled slowly.

Noticing the astonishment in my face, Miriam said, "Maybe it was someone else I saw."

"Perhaps he came looking for me. I should have taken the earlier train."

"It seems crazy for a man to come to visit his wife and not stick around until she gets here. And why did you catch the train when he has a car?" Miriam looked puzzled.

"He is traveling with the Colored League; maybe they had a break." Excuse after excuse for Simon was my only defense. I was exhausted from the thoughts of him. I felt weak at times because I couldn't seem to get this marriage thing right.

"Carrie, you are lucky to have a man who cares so much for you." Perhaps Miriam could not read between the lines.

"I suppose you are right," I said, doubting if it was me Simon was concerned about.

"I'd better get up the steps and unpack my clothes. Do you want to come with me?" I asked Miriam to get away from the two girls listening and snickering as we talked.

"Thanks, but I am going to sit around the fireplace for a while. I never know who I might meet coming through the front door. There are a couple more girls coming back today and both of them have older brothers." She smiled shyly.

I turned after climbing two of the stairs. "Thank you for letting me know Simon's in town."

"Well, it looked like him. And you needed to know he was around here," she mumbled. "I wouldn't want him to see what I saw a few minutes ago."

Shocked, my disposition had certainly changed. All the way up the stairs to my room, I was shaking my head from side to side, baffled about Simon. Why was he in Petersburg? He had been in Jefferson County when Momma came. It was as if he had another job I didn't know anything about. He should've been playing ball in New Orleans; at least that's what he'd told me. Unpacking my suitcase, I reflected back on Adam. I had to find him. I didn't want him to cross paths with Simon, because something dreadful was bound to happen.

CHAPTER 6

Adam came back to the boardinghouse around 7:30 on Tuesday morning. I was in the kitchen washing the dishes from breakfast. All of the girls living in the boardinghouse were either getting ready to make the eight-minute walk to school or go to a part-time job downtown, which was as rural as the country. My job at the boardinghouse was to make sure the kitchen was spotless, which meant putting away all the dishes, mopping the floor and setting the table for the next meal. Most days it was easy because women tend to clean up after themselves.

Adam stunned me when he walked into the kitchen. I turned around twice to make sure it was him. It was customary to receive guests in the parlor, but somehow, he had walked past the girls studying in the parlor straight into the kitchen and was staring me in the face. I was elated to see him because I had tossed and turned and even prayed Simon would not run into Adam. It was past 1 a.m. when I dozed off to sleep. I couldn't be sure of the time. When I woke up, Adam was on my mind. I was scared for his life.

"I thought you went home last night...thought you were going to catch the evening train back to Richmond." The train came twice a day and it was well occupied by the day workers of maids and lawn keepers. It was convenient having more than one train running between Richmond and Petersburg.

Adam smiled. "I changed my mind. I'll be going back later today."

"You are out early this morning," I said, rinsing the glass in my hand.

"I wanted to check on you before I went back home—make sure everything was good with you," he said, standing at the sink with me, watching me.

"Well, isn't that nice of you? You made sure I got here safely yesterday, and now you are back again," I said, drying the last dish, and swinging the dishtowel over my shoulder. "Would you like a cup of coffee? There is some still hot on the stove."

He pulled out a chair at the table and sat down.

I poured him a cup of coffee and sat down at the table across from him, mentally admiring his starched appearance. Instead of his usual calm demeanor, he seemed a bit anxious, maybe even a little nervous. He asked me, "Did Simon stop by here to see you last night?"

"What kind of question is that?" I responded.

"I thought I saw him last night when I was walking down the street towards my cousin's. He drove right past me. I thought he would turn around, but I don't think he saw me."

"What? I haven't seen or heard from him. He is supposed to be down in New Orleans," I replied, avoiding mentioning what Miriam had said.

"He is in town. I saw him with my own eyes. It looked like he was delivering something. He was carrying a paper box in his hands."

"That is strange. He didn't stop by here. I wonder if he knows I am in town. He told me he was going to be in New Orleans for a month or so. Now you are saying something different."

"Carrie, I hope you realize he is being dishonest with you. A real man wouldn't tell his wife lies like that. That man is not in New Orleans."

"It might have been someone else you saw." I quickly defended Simon.

"I know what he looks like, and I know the car he drives."

I gazed at him wondering what Simon was really up to. "There is no way Simon would be in this town and not stop by to see me." I wanted this to be true.

"He would if he was not alone."

"What are you saying?" I asked.

"Somebody else was in the car."

I sat straight up, and leaned in. "Are you sure? How could you see all of that in a passing car?"

"Because I saw him twice in one night: first driving down the street, and again when my cousin and I went to the bar. He came in there with a nice-looking brown woman. It was somebody I'm sure you know. "

Shaking my head, I said, "There is no way Simon is in town. He told me there is a man around who looks exactly like him. He said the man is the same height and color."

Adam frowned at my comment, as if my explanation was nonsense. "I couldn't leave you after seeing him. I wanted to hang around and make sure you were all right."

I became irritated. My eyes felt strange and my chest was heaving up and down. I wasn't sure what to say. I was tired of the stories about Simon.

"Carrie, the woman is not important. You should be more concerned about him sneaking in town without you knowing, and the secrets he might have."

"I want to know who he was with!" I shouted.

"Calm down, Carrie," he said, motioning with his hand as if to calm the waters.

He swallowed, and picked up his cup to sip the coffee. All the time, I could hear the clock ticking away on the mantle. When was he going to say something? I waited, biting my bottom lip. Adam just stared at me without speaking, and then he inhaled as to gain some nerve.

He held out his hand toward me and gestured. "Now, I want you to remain calm."

"I am calm," I said, my chest inflating and deflating with speed.

"It was your neighbor, Nadine, the one who lives across the street from you."

"Nadine, are you kidding me?! Did she see you?"

"No, I didn't stay in the bar. I told my cousin I'd catch up with him another time. I left before they noticed me and went back to my aunt's house. I thought about you all night. I didn't want you to be hurt. I really didn't know what to say to you. I just knew you deserved to know what is going on."

I felt a chill go through my body. I wanted to cry. My eyes welled up with water, but I fought the tears away. How could I be sad? I had come back to school with Adam and pretended like he was my man. I cared and maybe even loved Adam, yet my first love was Simon. Now, my fears had come true. He was with Nadine again. He said she was just a friend and nothing she could do would make him fall for her. The lying rascal...

"What should I do, Adam?"

"You will be all right," he said confidently.

"I think so," I agreed, wiping away the teardrops sliding down my cheeks with the back of my hand.

He peered at me from across the table and reached for my hand. "You know you will always have me."

I smiled.

Adam's eyes were penetrating. Concern had taken over his face.

His perfect smile was absent as he held his chin with his other hand. He was in deep thought.

"I am going back this afternoon, but if you want me to stick around another day, I can."

"I'll be fine—am too busy to think about Simon."

I washed the coffee cups we had used and left the kitchen. Adam followed close behind me. He helped me with my coat as I gathered my pad to take notes in class.

"I'm going to walk you to class. Then I'll head to the depot and wait for the train."

"The train will not be here for another hour."

"Waiting for a few minutes will not hurt me. And the cool wind is good for you. The ole folks claim the wind will blow away the germs in the air. I say the wind is good for troubles too."

"There are so many wives tales."

"I know, yet they make sense," he said.

It was cool, but the winds were calm. Even early, it appeared it was going to be a nice day. We walked across the street and down the road past the corner store to the school. It was good having Adam with me, but hectic knowing Simon was in town and could be somewhere watching my moves. On the other hand, he probably was preoccupied with Nadine, and the thought of me in school was far from his mind.

There was not a car in view. The only people in our path were the girls from the boardinghouse, including Miriam, who earlier warned me she had seen Simon too.

"Adam, I wasn't totally honest with you. Miriam saw Simon too. She told me last night after you left."

"Did she say where she saw him?"

"Yes, she said he was driving down the street—like he was leaving the boardinghouse."

"He should be mature about it all and tell you where he really is. Is he here or in New Orleans?"

"Let's not jump to conclusions," I pleaded.

"Carrie, please grow up. He is down here with another woman. There is nothing right about it. And by the way, he was carrying that box; he is up to no good."

"You are down here with me. I know he wouldn't like it if he knew about that."

"I guess he wouldn't," he answered, as if he didn't care.

"Let's forget about him for a moment. You are about to start a new semester," he said, taking my hand.

I smiled. "You are right. It is time to think about something new." I was growing up fast. I was a mother, wife and student. I enjoyed the experience and yet doubted myself much too often. Again, I had let Simon steal my joy.

A car drove past us and I trembled. "It's all right," Adam said. As we approached the largest building on the Normal School campus with tall pillars, like the ones at the antebellum homes and hotel I often admired, my heart began to be lonely thinking about Adam going back to Richmond and leaving me in Petersburg all by myself. Just before I went into the building, Adam pulled me close and whispered in my ear, "You have a man right here." Then he kissed me on the forehead and walked away.

CHAPTER 7

Miriam had somehow whittled her way into my life. No longer was she a student whom I shared a room with at the boardinghouse; she was becoming someone I valued as a friend. Ever since she had seen Simon driving his car past the boardinghouse and witnessed me kissing Adam passionately on the lips in the doorway, her involvement in my life was automatic. Her suspicions were ignited, and she longed to find out the truth.

"I don't know what is really going on with you, but you are different," Miriam said, standing with her hands on her narrow hips, her bright eyes searching my face for a reaction.

I shook my head and rolled my eyes at her comment; it was one I really didn't understand. What was so different about me? The only thing different in my mind was my living arrangements. I was living in Petersburg during the week and Richmond on the weekends.

Miriam was watching me like a hawk, her eyes darting back and forth wherever I moved. She was not going to let me get away without answering her questions. "What is going on with you? You seem different," she commented again.

"I'm the same person. I've got a few things on my mind."

"Well, something is going on," she said and put her hands on her hips again. "Simon is riding around town without stopping in on you and Adam is making frequent visits as if you are his woman. And that kiss the other night, what was that all about?"

"It was nothing, I told you. We got lost in the moment."

"Well, what is with Simon?"

"Hold your voice down," I warned her.

She whispered, "Well…"

"I don't know why he didn't stop by. He didn't know I was back," I said, tired of talking about him.

"I am concerned about you," she said, smacking her lips and whispering at the same time.

She finally sat down on the davenport beside me, folding her skirt underneath her as a proper Southern Belle would do. "Something is wrong when two people who are married do not tell each other where they are."

Her boldness should have struck a nerve with me, but it was the opposite. I sort of admired her asking me, rather than talking behind my back with the other girls, who loved to share gossip. Over the months, I had learned about one girl in the house being pregnant; another had run away from home; and one had two old men taking care of her. None of the gossip was important to me. So before I answered her, I had to think. I hung my head to gather my thoughts. When I finally decided to answer her, she sat waiting patiently with her arms crossed in front of her as if she had to know. "What do I know about marriage, Miriam?" I said. "You are making a lot of sense. I don't understand why there is so much distance between Simon and me. I can remember a time when we told each other just about everything."

"I'm sorry," she said. "I should be careful about my big mouth. My grandma warned me about my tongue. I didn't mean to hurt you. Perhaps I am like all the rest of people around me, nosy."

"It is okay. You've just said out loud what I have been thinking." What she said bothered me like all the rest of the insinuations about my husband. It was time to talk about things. I had tried to stay away from the questions, but there was no way I could. I didn't know what Simon was doing and neither did anyone else.

Miriam patted me on the leg. "It'll be all right, Carrie."

Tears welled up in my eyes and streamed down my cheeks. I wiped my eyes with the back of my hand. No one seemed to be watching. Miriam slid over and put her arm around me.

"Let's take a walk," Miriam suggested.

"It is cool outside. The wind is cold," I said, as she got up.

"I know, but it is sunny, and the sun is good for you. Just wrap your head up; you will be all right."

We both put on our coats and scarves and walked in the direction of the school. The wind felt good as it brazed my cheeks. Miriam seemed to enjoy it as well. She held her head high as if to let the breeze rub her face. After we had walked about two miles around the town and through the colored neighborhood, my head became clearer, and I had begun to appreciate the other things around me like the Normal School building and even the boardinghouse. My surroundings were symbols of hope. I wouldn't have traded that experience for anyone and especially Simon.

Our previous conversation was fresh in my thoughts. Although my thoughts were clearer, as we walked down the road toward the school building, my eyes scanned the Studebakers and a Model T Ford driving down the street. One of them was just like Simon's, but when I strained to see who the driver was, an old bald man peered back at me as if I was crazy. Simon obviously was long gone and nowhere in sight. I had a painful question of my own. Was he traveling with Nadine? Or did he come to Petersburg to meet her and the thought about me being in school never crossed his mind?

Miriam was a good person to talk to, but I didn't trust her enough to share everything going on with me. For two weeks nothing changed for me. Each day I expected Simon to show up at the boardinghouse. It didn't happen. All I did was read. I didn't even write any letters to mail home. I gave all my energy to my school work, and recalled how Mrs. Miller, my primary school teacher, had instilled in my head the desire to be educated. She'd said it was the only way colored folk could fit into the white man's world. Education was our freedom, and I loved school. With Momma caring for Robert, I felt secure, and skipped going home on the weekend. I didn't worry about him being a nuisance because I could tell by the sparkle in her mature eyes that she loved him and embraced him tenderly.

When I finally decided to go home, I felt in control. I had worked off the frustrations. I inhaled deeply when the train came around the curve, clacking and screeching. I got on and took a seat near the window in the colored section. I threw my head back and closed my eyes. I imagined teaching at a school in Richmond and even running my own school. I thought about all the things I desired in my life. I even thought about a life with Adam. I smiled when I stepped off the train in Richmond. For some unexplainable reason, seeing my family was not first on my mind. I wanted to see Adam, who had not been back to Petersburg since he'd left. Instead, I walked right past his tenement house and down the street without stopping. I turned onto Clay Street, crossed over by The Deuce, where Ms. Pearl sang, and continued home.

Stepping onto the porch, Momma swung the door wide open as if she had been waiting for me. She immediately handed Robert to me. "Your baby needs to know who his momma is," she said, not giving me time to put my suitcase down.

Robert smiled at me. I hugged him so tightly, he started to whimper. When I sat him down, he grinned and grabbed Momma's dress and hung on to her.

"It is so nice to be home," I said, taking a seat at the kitchen table.

Momma stood with Robert holding onto her dress tail. "I was wondering when you would be coming home. It seems like you've been gone for weeks."

"It's only been two weeks. Did Robert give you trouble?" I asked.

"No, he was a good chile; I'm just not used to being inside the house so much. It is not much to do around here. I like being here, but miss my little day job working for Mrs. Ferguson. I know by now she is having a fit. And, of course, I hope Carl is feeding the hogs and chickens."

"Mrs. Ferguson needs to learn to do things herself. I don't like the way she treats you anyhow. And Carl can do things as well as Papa could."

Momma sat down. "Well, I'm used to her," she said, "Her ways used to bother me when I first started working for her, but now I know she don't mean any harm. She just don't know how to treat colored peoples."

"She is just plain ole mean. And she doesn't like colored people, either. She treats you like a slave, Momma."

"Now she was the first one to come check on us after your papa died. She was so sweet."

I refused to comment. Mrs. Ferguson had always treated Momma and me like we were her servants. I regretted Momma working for her, yet it was a good way for her to get out of the house. Farming and housework were possibly the most mundane tasks of all kinds of work. Listening to Mrs. Ferguson give orders and watching her run her hands along the mantle, making sure we didn't forget to dust, was the only memory I really had of her. With the exception of her ruby-red lipstick, she was nonexistent to me, and I wished Momma felt the same.

"Were you able to get any shopping done?"

"I left Robert with Mrs. Hall once to do the shopping. When I stopped in the corner store, Kindred, Herman's brother, was there. He scared me to death."

"What did he do to you?" I asked.

"He didn't do nothing to me. He just looked so much like Herman, I thought I had seen a ghost."

"Did you talk to him?"

"I never met the man, yet he knew who I was. He asked about the child."

"Momma, he is just like his brother. I've never seen twins who looked so much alike. Why is he so concerned about Robert?"

"He is just trying to be family like. What puzzles me is he is the spitting image of Herman. He evens sounds like him when he talks."

"I don't think Herman is dead. I think the man we call Kindred is Herman."

"It can't be. I dressed him and helped the undertaker put him in the box. It is not Herman."

"Momma, it is strange how he has ended up in the same town as Pearl Brown, Herman's former mistress."

"Maybe Pearl followed him here."

"I doubt it. Ms. Pearl said she just wants to sing and Richmond offered everything she was looking for and it is real close to Washington, D.C."

"Chile, Pearl will tell you anything. She couldn't have Herman so she went after his brother."

"Momma, Mr. Camm was no one to have."

"Chile, all of us have our faults."

I shook my head. I couldn't believe she was still defending him. It was why I didn't tell her what he had done to me. She would have taken up for him. It was something about that man she loved. Nobody could understand what the attraction really was.

"Did he say anything else to you?"

"He told me I was looking nice," Momma mumbled, with a sly grin on her face.

"Did he act like he knew you?"

"No, he was just a nice man, I tell you."

I bit my tongue, and suffered because I wanted to explode. Momma had once again, in my mind, been fooled by Herman Camm. No matter what he had done, she seemed to have forgotten about all the lies he had told, and now pretending to be a twin brother was an all-time low. It was the subtle blush, and the twinkle in her eyes that had me worried. Immediately, I recalled how she had sashayed into the house after going to Washington, D.C., when Papa was on his deathbed. She'd had a peculiar grin on her face and none of us could understand why. Soon afterward, Herman Camm showed up.

"Momma, please listen to me; this man might be Herman," I explained, gesturing with my hands.

"Chile, I was there when they put him down six feet in the ground. Herman is not around here. He is gone to glory, I tell you."

I couldn't believe my ears, so I got up and poured myself a glass of water. She didn't say anything. Robert followed behind me and waited like a little puppy to have a drink. He was getting big. His features were changing and for a moment, he seemed to resemble Herman Camm. I forced that thought out of my mind.

I picked up my suitcase. "Momma, I'm tired; I am going to take a nap."

"All right," she said, and began to hum. Then she said, "Simon ain't coming home, is he?"

"Why are you asking, Momma?"

"I just have a feeling things are not good. You are home now, and your husband has been gone a long time."

"It has only been two weeks."

"I know, and the strange thing is, I haven't seen Nadine since I've been here."

"Oh, she is around."

"It is strange that she is also missing. I haven't seen her or the children."

I inhaled to keep from getting upset. "He is coming home soon, Momma. New Orleans is quite a distance."

I went into the bedroom where Robert and I lay down and took a nap. On Saturday, I spent the entire day with Robert. We walked downtown and I took him to visit my childhood friend Hester. Hester and he had the best time laughing and rolling a ball on the floor. I hoped Simon would be home when we returned, but he wasn't there. I caught the train back to Petersburg on Sunday.

CHAPTER 8

Seemingly, I had chosen the best weekend ever to come home from the Normal School. Everybody, including Momma, was talking about the rumors floating around. They said Bessie Smith was in town. The man who owned the corner feed, seed and everything else store said, "People are saying they saw Bessie Smith drive into town late last night. I'm going to be there front and center when she walks up on the stage." The cobbler said Bessie Smith came with two car loads of people and they got rooms at the colored hotel. It was more like an oversized house than a hotel. Now that was news. I couldn't wait to see if it was really true.

"I heard Bessie is here and I want to go to the club tonight!" I excitedly told Momma after handing her the pork sausage I'd purchased from the corner store, along with the ten pounds of flour.

"Chile, I want to hear Bessie too, but I know it is best to stay away from places like the club."

"Clubs are not bad; it is the people who go there that cause the problems."

"I don't go to places like that," Momma said, and threw her nose up in the air, shaking her head.

Immediately, it came to mind how, according to Aunt Bessie, Momma had visited the club in Washington, D.C., the night she met Herman Camm. And whenever Aunt Bessie mentioned it, Momma would stop her. "Hush yo' mouth, Bessie, telling them lies on me."

Aunt Bessie would just smile and say, "You know the truth, Mae Lou, and I know the truth too."

So I pushed the point. "Didn't you go to see Ms. Pearl one night a long time ago?" I asked her.

Her eyes rolled around and her head followed so fast, I stepped back. "It was the first and last time I set foot in any place to see that floozy Pearl Brown!" she yelled. "We were in Washington, and that is where everybody go on Friday night. Now decent people down here don't go to places like that, and you shouldn't, either. Bessie should have kept her big mouth shut putting all this foolishness in yo' head."

Making sense of her visit did not mean much to me, so I didn't say another word. "Momma, Simon and I love to go listen to her sing. And you know she can sing. There is not much else around here for us to do."

"I never had a hard time finding things to do around the house. I took care of my home and it was more important than hanging out in joints with floozies."

"I'm different. I try not to spend too much time judging others. I'm not perfect, either; nobody is, Momma."

"I didn't raise you to hang out in any bar listening to Bessie Smith and Pearl Brown. The both of them have a shady past. Everybody likes Bessie because she nasty and common acting."

"I don't hang in bars alone. Even Ms. Maggie Walker, the richest colored lady around here, comes to the club."

"Something is wrong with Maggie too. She should be setting an example for people around here."

"Momma, it is no harm in enjoying music."

"Well, I didn't come up here to watch Robert while you hang in nightclubs," she said, folding laundry she had been ironing in the kitchen.

"I thought you came because you wanted to help me."

"I will watch him while you go to school and do some of your chores, but I will not take care of him while you run to nightclubs without your husband. A lady ain't got no business in places where Pearl Brown sings."

"I just don't see the harm in listening to someone sing."

"You are still young. You can't see a lot of things. It is up to me to tell you what I know."

At that point, I dared to tell her I had been at the club the night Willie, Ms. Pearl's husband, was gunned down by the white man whom Ms. Pearl is often seen with. For some unforeseen reason, he pulled out a gun and shot Willie. I will always believe it was because he loved Ms. Pearl so much; after all, she was Willie's wife. I would never let her know about Simon and me crawling on the floor praying to get out of there without harm. My momma was not the type of person you could tell much to, and no matter how much we talked, there were still many things I knew that with all her wisdom, she could not handle.

"You do whatever you want, Chile, but I am not going to keep the baby."

Her words were solid. I shook my head and clucked my tongue. She was now acting like the Jefferson County momma, the one who lived in a small space and only saw things from one point of view.

All evening she stared at me with an evil eye as I ironed the dress I was wearing to the club. Momma didn't say anything, and yet occasionally, I'd hear her make a comment under her breath.

"She need to keep herself right here with you, little boy," she said to Robert, and he returned a smile as if he knew what she was talking about.

Momma sat in the soft chair in the bedroom, and sank her head back into the pillow. Occasionally, she would peek over at me laying out my skirt and blouse and shake her head. I couldn't fathom what was so bad about going to hear one of the most famous singers of all times. Folks were going to be there from all the counties around, even Washington, D.C.

"Momma, would you like to come with me?"

"Chile, I have told you. I ain't going to hear nothing Pearl Brown is singing. Now, if Bessie Smith was at a club alone, I probably would consider going just once. I don't like clubs and places like that. The people that hang in there are from the low places on this earth. They come in there to find a solution to their problems by drinking and acting a fool."

"The rumors are she is going to stop in the place where Ms. Pearl performs, and they might do a song together."

"I am so tired of hearing Pearl's name. Now, Carrie, I told you I am not going to see about no chile while you are out tonight."

I glanced over at her and shook my head. "No, Ma'am. Mrs. Hall is going to watch him for me. You will have the house all to yourself. "

"I can't believe you going down there with those people. Chile, you just don't want to learn. You are even foolish enough to take Robert downstairs for the night. You are not the same chile I raised to have good values and manners. You act like you ain't never been to church."

"Momma, I am going with Hester. If you want to go, you can. Please stop putting Ms. Pearl down. She was not by herself, and you know Mr. Camm was the real problem. I am a good girl, Momma!"

Immediately, Momma started to hum. She often did it when she was tired of what she was hearing. I knew she was tired, and so was I. She had a negative attitude about everybody but that awful Herman Camm. It was probably the reason it took me so long to tell anybody about what he was doing to me. I was afraid she would not believe me, and it turned out she didn't.

Hester met me at 7 p.m. I was dressed up. I had on my dropped waist skirt and white blouse, silk stockings, cinnamon-pressed powder on my face, and a shiny red lipstick. I looked at myself in the mirror and smiled. I liked the way face powder made me look. I looked older and more mature, and the tiny pimple on my cheek was barely noticeable. I felt beautiful. I had learned how to apply the powder from Miriam. She always wore it to class with a little lipstick.

Going away to school had been great for me. I had learned how to blend in with the other women. I no longer stuck out in the crowd as the little country girl wearing the potato sack skirts and hair locked in braids. I now looked like everybody else. I rolled my hair every night with strips from a brown paper sack, or I would put a few pin clips in it. Miriam had said the face powder and new hair style enhanced my appearance, even though she thought I was naturally cute.

It was strange meeting Hester, my best friend, instead of Simon. He had been gone for a long month now. Every day I expected him to return home. I had spent the morning sitting in the bay window gazing out at the blowing trees, expecting to see Simon drive down the street. Of course he didn't ever show up. I supposed whatever had his attention was more important than Robert and me. Tonight I would let the rich sounds of Bessie Smith and Pearl Brown take my mind away from thinking about Simon. Every time I peered across the street at Nadine's house, it appeared lifeless, and I wondered if she was home or still in the company of my husband. I hoped I would never catch them.

Hester was standing on the corner waiting for me with her arms crossed. She stood propped up against the building facing the side of the nightclub. She was spiffy, dressed in a peach-colored dress, nude silk stockings and her long hair loose and curled on the ends. Her face was gleaming from the pressed powder and rouge. Actually, she looked like a grown woman and she had the attention of a man standing across the street who aimed to get her attention by whistling at her. She just stood there smiling. I felt we both appeared older than usual. Lipstick and pressed powder had that effect on most women.

When Hester wrote to tell me she was moving to Richmond from Washington, D.C., my eyes lit up. She had been my best friend for as long as I could remember. She was the one person I trusted with most everything. Having her in Richmond was the best thing that could have happened to me, and she moved right around the corner. She had this way of looking out for me, as if she was the older sister, although we were the same age. I could remember the way she reacted when I finally told her I was pregnant. She immediately went into action trying to help me figure a way out of my situation. After she left Jefferson County, she would write me, encouraging me to get out of Jefferson as soon as I could. "The world is so much bigger. When you get away from country Jefferson County, you will finally be able to spread your wings. I am so glad I'm gone," she wrote.

So as we walked side by side down the street toward the club, I felt a burst of confidence having her with me. Men tipped their hats and we glanced at each other, giggling because of the admiration. One man whistled, and we both turned our heads. When we made it to the club, we both hesitated and smiled. We were finally doing some of the things we'd quietly planned in primary school.

Cars of all sorts pulled up to the entrance of the club—Studebakers, Model T's and Buicks. People got out dressed nicely from head to toe. The men had on suits and Fedoras, and the women were dressed in chiffon dresses and silk hose. Hester and I were dressed exactly the same way. We found a place in the line, and anxiously waited to go in. We all patiently waited to get a seat and to engage in what was supposed to be the best show ever held in Richmond. The whispers about Bessie Smith coming had everyone excited to get a glimpse of the woman whose success Ms. Pearl Brown wanted to imitate.

Everything appeared normal. The same people I'd seen in the club before were seated in their favorite places. This Saturday, it was extra crowded. I'd overheard one man say folk were being turned around at the door. Hester and I were happy to be early. We took special notice in watching the people arrive and seeing the types of fashions the women wore. We sat in the middle, halfway to the front of the stage. I liked being close to the door too. We could see who came and left without anybody noticing we were being nosy. I also felt safer knowing I could get out quickly in case a brawl broke out. There were no more available tables, just folks standing around the perimeter of the wall, most of them smiling and chatting about how they would be able to recognize Bessie when she came through the door. One man exaggerated saying she was nearly six feet tall. Everybody knew about the tough woman with the electrifying voice. We believed she was better than Ma Rainey. However, our Pearl Brown was up-and-coming. Folks said she was prettier and better than Bessie, and could outsing her as well.

"I'm so glad we decided to come here," Hester said, rotating her hat brim, making sure it was perfect. It was sassily tilted to the side.

"It is crowded tonight. Everybody is here," I said, glancing around and gauging the crowd.

"Did you ever go to a club in D.C.?" I asked Hester.

"No, I never did. John never took me to one, and women are not supposed to be seen in them alone."

"I'm glad you are in Richmond now. I've never been here without Simon. He is the one who told me about this place. It is a bit eerie being here without him. But I see plenty of women in here alone."

"I've been to the theater by myself," Hester said. "It was a bit boring compared to this."

The music was louder than normal. The tiny quartet stood on stage playing while the crowd moseyed in and took their seats. It was packed to capacity, the bartender rushing from one side of the bar to the other filling their drinks. The excitement was elevated. People were fidgety, moving from place to place. Several men walked around the perimeter as if they had been paid to keep watch. All of us were so anxious, we could not keep still. So eyes darted from place to place trying to be the first to catch a glimpse of Bessie, Pearl or both. The normal, dull mirror behind the bar was sparkling clear; even the patrons seated at the bar could get a good look at them coming toward the stage. After a short while, Pearl strutted from the back of the room up to the stage and grabbed the microphone. The crowd roared at the sight of her. The men stood smiling like Cheshire cats and began clapping so loudly, the palms of their hands were red. She acknowledged their applause, and held her hand out to the crowd. The applause grew stronger. She did not disappoint them. She started out with a boisterous piece and everybody was bouncing heads. It was a little different than ever before. She seemed to want to give the audience a show they would not forget.

Just as we were all clapping and swaying back and forth to the sounds of the infamous Pearl Brown, in walked Bessie Smith. We were so involved in the show Pearl was displaying, that we barely noticed Bessie being there until she strutted toward the stage, escorted by two very handsome men. At first sight of her, the clapping became louder. Ms. Smith had them shouting. She finished one song with Pearl and then came off the stage. She went to the bar where the bartender offered her a drink. When she took the drink, she held it up high toward the ceiling, and then she downed it like a man. The crowd roared in thunderous applause. Hester whispered to me, "That was not ladylike." I couldn't help bursting out laughing. Afterward, Bessie and her crew left the club without speaking to anyone. It didn't seem to matter because she'd given us a taste of her blues.

Hester and I couldn't stop clapping even though Bessie was out of the door.

"This is the best show ever," Hester said, clapping so hard the palms of her hands were red.

"She let us know she could sing. Ms. Pearl sang like a songbird too."

Hester smiled. "You know it feels a little strange being here without a man."

"Simon is usually here with me," I commented.

"Is that Simon over there?"

I turned to see who it was and the man Hester was pointing at was already out of sight. Whoever she saw had moved so quickly in the crowd, I could not even catch a glimpse. It was a relief to know Kindred were nowhere to be found. The white man Ms. Pearl left with some nights was mingling at the bar.

Hester and I started toward the door, when I glanced at the crowd still lingering and saw a man leave who favored Simon from behind. I tried to catch him. I ran toward the exit, and called his name, but the man did not turn around and there were too many people between us for me to get a good look.

"This has been a great night," Hester commented.

"Ms. Bessie Smith was wonderful. She sure surprised us with her entrance."

Hester and I separated at the corner. Even though it was not summer, it was a mild night and the temperature was around sixty-five degrees. I took off my heels and ran barefoot the entire distance home. I couldn't take any chances, not knowing who was lurking around Jackson Heights.

CHAPTER 9

The house was as dark as a starless sky when I got home, and the door was unlocked and partially opened. Immediately, fear rose up in me. I grabbed the baseball bat in the corner of the kitchen and shut the door behind me. I tipped from the kitchen to the bedroom with the bat held high in my hands, my heart thumping in my chest. I was going to find out what was going on.

Momma was lying on the davenport with a quilt thrown across her. She heard me walk into the room and rose up. "Why do you have that bat in your hands?" she asked.

"Momma, the door was unlocked."

"Go on to bed, Chile; ain't nobody in here."

"Why is the door unlocked?" I asked again.

She didn't say anything. She turned over on the davenport, with her back facing me. It was unusual for her to leave the door unlocked, especially since she didn't trust people from the city. "They are too slick for me, and they take and don't know hard work," she'd often said. We were not in Jefferson County where the nearest neighbor was a quarter-mile away. Everybody there left doors unlocked and windows up on summer nights.

When I walked into my bedroom, to my surprise, Simon was lying across the bed with nothing on but his undershorts, waiting for me. Simon had his arms behind his head and a wide smile across his face.

"Come on in here," he commanded me.

At first sight I shook my head and walked into the room smiling. The closer I got to the bed, the more thoughts started invading my head. Was he at the club tonight? I had to know. When did he really come home?

"Did I see you at the club tonight?" I asked.

"Carrie, can I answer your questions later? Come over here. I haven't seen you in over a month."

The lamp was casting shadows on the wall. Even though the lights were low, I didn't feel the mood it was supposed to bring. As I walked toward the bed, all I thought of was that my husband had been deceiving me. He had been seen everywhere, but at home. When I got to the foot of the bed, I paused before sitting down. I wasn't sure I wanted to be in the same room, much less the same bed with him.

"Why are you standing there? Come sit beside me," he said, patting the bed for me to sit down.

"I have got to change into my night clothes," I said, unbuttoning my shirt.

"You look nice. Where have you been?"

"I was at the club."

He smiled at what I said, but did not comment. Did he care I was at the club, or did he already know? I thought a woman was supposed to go to the club with her man.

"Sit down right here," he insisted, patting a spot on the bed again.

I sat down with my back toward Simon and kicked off my shoes. I reached down and neatly placed them together on the floor. Simon placed his hand on my back and began to knead it with his fingertips. I didn't react.

"Why are you acting like I'm a stranger? You got your back towards me. I've been gone for over a month; surely you are glad to see me."

I turned around and gazed into his eyes. He smiled and held out his arms for me to lie in. I slid closer to him and lay down beside him fully dressed. He coaxed me down into his muscular arms. And quietly I snuggled in, as usual.

"What is wrong with you?" he asked, wrapping his strong arms around me.

I couldn't believe he didn't know what was wrong. I stared into his beautiful almond eyes searching for evidence of deception and waited to see what he would say next. As I thought, he didn't say a word. Finally, I pulled away from his arms and rose up off the bed. I sat on the edge of the bed. "I've got to take my clothes off," I said and began to undress.

I finished unbuttoning my blouse. I hung my skirt and blouse on clothes racks in the closet and searched for the pink gown Momma had made me for my sixteenth birthday.

Being beside Simon triggered warmth all over my body. Simon waited patiently for me to crawl in bed beside him. Once I was lying in his arms, he kissed me. I wanted to pull back, but instead, I let him lay his lips on mine. He started to pull up my nightgown, but I couldn't let him. I quickly pulled it back down.

"What is wrong with you?" he asked me. I could see the scowl on his face, and the sudden irritation.

"You haven't been here," I answered him.

"You know where I've been. I've been down in New Orleans playing baseball, and we stopped over in Atlanta for a few days."

I bit my lip and shook my head. "Are you sure that's where you've been?"

He sat up in the bed. And I did the same thing.

"Carrie, I've warned you about listening to people. I've been down south. I can tell somebody done put some more lies in your head."

"Simon, people are seeing you everywhere. Somebody even saw you in Petersburg. Was that a lie too?" I boldly asked.

"I haven't been near Petersburg. I don't know why they are always telling you things about me. They ought to find something to do and stay out of my damn business." The words came out choppy as if he was a stutterer. I could tell he was uncomfortable by the tone of his voice and how he raised it at the mention of Petersburg.

"I just don't understand why people would want to lie on you, Simon."

"They will, Carrie, I tell you. People are always creating things. I rushed home to see my wife and this is what I get," he argued.

"Simon, people are seeing you around town. Even tonight somebody recognized you at the club."

"Ain't nobody seen me at the damn club. I wasn't near the club. I've been driving all night trying to get home to see my family, and this is what I get."

"Simon, let's not argue about this," I said, to calm him down.

He put his arm around my shoulder. I wanted to pull away, but instead, I slid back into his arms, bewildered, but not fooled.

He smiled. "Now that's more like it."

All of a sudden, I felt conquered. I forced a grin. He kissed me hard on the lips. I loved his scent, and just the touch of his skin next to mine made me weak.

"Why are you all wrapped up?" he asked, attempting to lift my gown over my head.

"Momma is here," I whispered.

"I know. The door is closed; she can't hear us."

Simon ran his hand up my thigh. The warmth of his touch caused me to tremble. Just as he ran his fingers between my legs, I closed them tight.

"I can't, Simon; not tonight," I said, knocking his hand away.

"Don't let all that nonsense come between us," he begged.

"I won't if you don't," I shot back.

I closed my eyes and took a deep breath. Simon pulled me close. I wanted to give in, but instead, I fought my own natural desires, turned my back to him and dozed off to sleep. It was the principle of it all. How could he lie about so many things in one breath? Everybody had seen him. I knew they all couldn't be lying. Even though it was hard for me to resist him, I had to be strong for one night. I closed my eyes, knowing I wanted him real bad.

Momma woke up early the next morning. She wrapped her apron around her waist and began preparing eggs, buttermilk biscuits and bacon. The aroma was tantalizing and I patiently waited to enjoy her cooking. Simon was quiet as if something was on his mind. Momma was humming her gospel songs as usual when she cooked, and singing notes out of tune. The only person missing was Robert who was still at the Halls—the result of Momma taking a stand against Pearl, Bessie, and the club and refusing to take care of Robert while I was out.

After everyone was served, Momma sat down to eat. "How was the show last night?"

"It was nice."

"I can't believe you went to the club alone," Simon commented.

"I didn't."

"Who did you go with?"

"Hester." Last night, he had never bothered to ask.

"How was the music? Did Bessie perform?" Momma asked.

"Bessie sang one song with Ms. Pearl. They sounded so good together."

Momma shook her head. "Bessie can sing, but folks say she live worse than Pearl. The two of them together, Lawd have mercy! Neither one of 'em go to church."

Her comments disturbed me so much I was forced to bite my tongue.

"I wish I had made it back in time to come to the show," Simon said, with a straight face; yet his eyes said something different. I couldn't believe my ears.

The food was tasty as expected, yet both of the comments had my nerves a bit rattled. I wanted to say something to both Momma and Simon. Momma's negative comments seemed to surface whenever anybody mentioned Ms. Pearl. And now she was talking about Miss Bessie Smith too. I didn't agree with their lifestyles, but both of them could sing.

I told Momma and Simon about the crowd the night before. Simon listened as if he had not been there, even though he had been seen in the crowd.

"I wanted to be there," Simon kept mumbling.

We were enjoying the meal, and passionately discussing Ms. Pearl and Bessie when there was a hard knock on the door.

"Now who can that be this early in the mo'ning?" Momma asked, getting up and wiping her hands on her apron.

When she opened the door, the tone of her voice changed.

"Hi, what can we do for you?" she asked firmly.

"I want to borrow a cup of sugar," Nadine said. I cringed. The frequent sugar visits were getting to be a habit.

Momma turned toward us. "The neighbor wants a cup of sugar." Neither of us said anything. After a moment, Momma said, "Come on in. I will get you some. Did you bring a cup with you?"

"No, Ma'am. I plain forgot," she said.

Momma cut her eyes at me. Nadine stepped inside the door and a smile rolled across her face.

"Hi, Simon!" she said, waving, and then added, "Oh, hi, Carrie." It came out like she'd forgotten about me. I glanced over at Simon, and immediately he took a sip of his coffee. He kept his eyes on the coffee he was drinking, never looking up. He appeared annoyed; I could see the tightening in his cheeks. Momma stood at the counter dipping sugar into a paper sack for Nadine. Nadine as usual was boldly staring at Simon as if I was not in the room. He inhaled and shifted his eyes toward Momma, who was also waiting to see what was going to happen.

"Nadine, this is the first time I've seen you since I've been in town. Where have you been?" Momma asked.

"Well, I sorta wasn't around here for a while," she answered, slyly gazing over at Simon.

Momma quickly came back, "Where have you been?"

"I've got some people down near Petersburg. Are you almost done with the sugar?" Nadine asked, as if all of a sudden she was in a hurry.

Momma handed her the brown paper bag containing a cup of sugar. Nadine grabbed the bag and took off without saying another word. Simon did not move, yet there was an aura of mystique on his face. He coughed to clear his throat, but nothing came out.

"I told you she didn't have any manners. She strutted out of here without saying thank you," Momma said, with a disgusted look on her face.

"I'm just glad she is gone," I said, peering over at Simon who had his hand around his chin as if he was in a deep thought.

"I thought the girl had moved. I haven't seen her or the children the entire time I've been here."

Momma said exactly what I was thinking. It appeared as if Nadine and Simon had the same schedule and it bothered me. The conversation at the table almost completely diminished with each step Nadine took back across the street. First there was chatter and now total silence. Her presence had changed the entire atmosphere of my home. Simon's eyes had become slits and he was staring at the wall while Momma was standing at the sink mumbling about her rude departure. "That girl worries me," Momma said, shaking her head, "She is trouble." Momma was a professional at getting on my bad side, and today more so than ever. I wanted to choke her. Instead, I finished my breakfast and excused myself. It was time to get Robert from Mrs. Hall and bring him home.

CHAPTER 10

Although spring was around the corner, the winter chill still had the ground frozen stiff. The ground crunched underneath me with each step I took. I had gotten tired of being inside the house, so I took a walk down toward the club in hopes of running into Adam. I had been home all day snuggled around the fireplace waiting for my husband who seemed to always take his time coming home. Amazingly, some of the town was just finding out about Bessie Smith being in town, and they lined up to see her, only to meet disappointment. Simon swore he had a hard time convincing the eager crowd that Bessie Smith had come and was long gone.

Walking had become a means to clear my head, especially when I was upset. I would walk for as long as it took to clear my head. At times I'd get lost in the scenery, the height of the trees and how the birds flew in a "V formation." At times, I would walk behind a couple holding hands and I would get a little jealous inside. But I thought it was a beautiful thing—love, that is. As I approached the club, I could see smoke coming out of the chimney, billowing and dissipating in air. As I walked up on the club, something compelled me to step inside. Simon had said at the breakfast table that he had business to settle with the owner. I wasn't sure who was the real owner of the club because the white man who had murdered Willie was there watching over Ms. Pearl and so was the tall, quiet, colored man I thought was the owner.

I turned the doorknob and the door was unlocked. I walked into the club as if I worked there. I glanced around and didn't see anybody but the bartender who seemed to never go home. He was wiping down the bar and arranging the shot glasses in a format only he could understand. He'd lined them on each side behind the bar. I walked over to him, and slid onto the bar stool. A strange place for me, since sitting at a bar was where single women sat who were hoping to be picked up for the night.

"We're not open, Ma'am," the bartender said.

"I was hoping to catch Ms. Pearl in here."

"I think she is in the back," he said, peering at the door in the back of the room.

"I'll go back there."

"Now wait a minute. She doesn't like people looking in on her before the show."

"I'm from her hometown; I don't think she will mind," I assured him.

"Well, you go on your own…"

It was a strange feeling acting like a grownup. Richmond had been the city of changes for me. I had remembered being afraid to be seen in a place like this. Momma still called it a place for floozies and drunks. I see it as a place to get to know people. When Mrs. Maggie Walker was at the club, I felt I was amongst royalty, and everybody treated her in that manner. There were many other business owners who frequented the club; some I recognized and some I didn't. It seemed to me like the entire community visited the club at some time or another. It was too early for action yet I searched around for a glimpse of Simon and even questioned the bartender before going in the back to see Ms. Pearl.

"Is Simon here?"

"I haven't seen him today. He will probably be in later, though. I thought you wanted to see Ms. Pearl."

I smiled at his comment. I got up from the bar stool and walked toward the back room. The times I had been in the club, Ms. Pearl was always up front. This was the first time I had been in the back room, although I had seen people come out of the back while I was there, mainly the workers, the white man, and other mysterious-looking folks. I'd often wondered what was going on in the room, since folks were always coming and going.

I heard voices coming from the room, even before I walked up. It was a jovial giggle being shared by Ms. Pearl and a man. I almost turned around, but instead, I tapped lightly on the door.

"Who is it?" Ms. Pearl asked from the other side of the door.

"It's me... Carrie."

"Hold on a minute, baby," she said.

I waited patiently for a few seconds before the door cracked open.

"Come on in," she said, without me seeing her.

I stepped inside the compact room. There was a davenport and a table with a kerosene lamp and a drink on it. Ms. Pearl was sitting on the davenport. After I was inside the door, it was closed behind me. When I heard the door close, I glanced over my shoulder and there was Kindred Camm standing in the room. Immediately, I began to get worried. I started to tremble. My hands turned wet from my nerves.

"What's wrong?" Ms. Pearl asked.

"Can I talk to you alone?" I asked.

"Sure you can," she said, looking at Kindred. "Give us a few minutes."

"No problem," Kindred said, and added, "nice to see you again, Carrie."

I cringed when he said my name. Ms. Pearl saw the frown roll over my face. He seemed to know me and we had never been introduced.

"You all right?" she asked.

"I'm fine," I said, waiting for Kindred to leave, and shut the door. My knees were wobbly.

"You seem upset, Carrie. What is wrong? Did Kindred say something to you?"

"No, Ma'am. I just can't believe he is Mr. Camm's brother. He looks so much like his brother, it is scary."

She paused before speaking. "Me, either, Chile. Have a seat."

It took me a few seconds to gather myself before I could talk to Ms. Pearl.

"Take your time."

I inhaled. I closed my eyes. I took exaggerated deep breaths, and finally got my heart to slow down and beat normally. It had felt as if my heart was going to jump out of my chest. When I finally contained my emotions and realized I had let Kindred steal my joy, I got back on track. I was in a state of panic. "Ms. Pearl, I have several things I want to talk to you about."

"I can see something is weighing you down. Sit down and rest for a minute."

I sat down in a wooden chair facing her. "You said I could stop by at any time, right?"

"Yes, you are always welcome to come by to see me."

I glanced over at the door. "Simon is supposed to be here, right? Have you seen him?"

"Honey, he is in and out. I haven't seen him today."

"Ms. Pearl, do you like Simon?"

"Now what kind of question is that?" she asked, studying me, and sipping on the drink that was on the table.

"I'm having a hard time understanding men."

"They are all hard to understand. You ain't by yourself."

"You sort of know men."

She shook her head. "Yes, I sort of know men. Now just ask me what you came in here for."

"Well, Simon is in and out of town. People see him places and he is denying it is true. Was he here the other night when Bessie Smith was in town?"

"Simon knows a lot of people. He even knows Bessie. I can say for sure he was here because he is one of the people who drove her into town."

As I heard this, I could not do anything but bite my bottom lip and listen. "How does he know so many people?"

"Now that is something you need to talk to him about, Chile."

"Do you know about him playing ball?"

"Everybody knows he wants to play with the colored boys and the best, Pete Hill. He can talk about baseball all day long."

"He is always traveling with the Colored League."

"Yes, folks say he can really hit that ball too," Ms. Pearl said.

Most everybody knew of Pete Hill and Rube Foster. They were the best baseball players ever. Every colored player in Virginia was trying to hit like Pete Hill and gain the same kind of fame. After hearing so much about them, I, too, wanted to meet the infamous Pete Hill and his manager, Rube Foster. But I knew my Simon was holding some kind of secret by the manner in which Ms. Pearl answered my questions and twirled her hair at the same time.

"Ms. Pearl, how can I get the truth from my husband?"

"Just stand up to him. Tell him you know he is not telling you everything, and as his wife, you are entitled to know. That's what I would tell my man. Now keep in mind that Simon is a business-man," she said with a sly grin.

"Can you tell me what's going on?"

"No, it is not up to me. He should tell you, and don't be a fool for him or anybody else, now. You are young, but don't be stupid."

I could tell by the way she expressed herself and the seriousness in her eyes, she was also concerned. I don't think it was about me, but what I might find out. I wasn't finished. I didn't know how to ask this one, but I had to say something to her.

"Ms. Pearl, is Kindred Camm really Herman's brother?"

"Well, Chile, he say he is. He is the spitting image of Herman. I am trying to believe Kindred, but the more he is around me, the more he looks and acts like his brother. Some twins are just alike. If I notice anything different, I will certainly say it. Right now, he is all right. You can't be too sure of nothing these days. Colored men love to tell lies, Chile."

"Thanks, Ms. Pearl," I said and got up to leave.

"You've got a whole lot on your mind. Remember you are still a young girl. Don't let stuff keep you from enjoying your life. Now where is that young man you came here with?"

Immediately, I felt bad. I had been asking questions about my husband and all the time Ms. Pearl was also reading me. When she asked about Adam, I knew she knew about us.

"I hope to see him soon."

"If I was you, I'd keep him around. I see the way he looks at you."

"I'm married, Ms. Pearl."

"So is Simon... Just take care of yourself. You have a life too."

As I stood up to leave, I couldn't help thinking about Kindred who was outside the door, somewhere. Nobody really knew anything about Kindred. When he first came to town, it was to find his brother's killer. Now all he did was hang around Ms. Pearl. On my way to the front door, I saw him sitting at the bar holding a drink of sorts in his hand. It was the same color as the dark liquor Herman used to drink. They were so much alike. It was as if he didn't have anywhere to be. He saw me and a smile ripped across his face. I glanced over at him with a nasty scowl on my face.

"Have a good day," he said as I headed out the door. I didn't mumble a word. I looked back to see if his eyes were following me. Instead, he had gotten up and was walking back toward the room where Ms. Pearl was. I was relieved. He was not like his brother after all, gazing at young girls inappropriately and stalking them.

I walked right into Simon's chest as I was exiting the club. His eyes nearly popped out of his head when he saw me. He immediately stopped right in his tracks. He put down the box he had in his arms, which appeared to be heavy. The bartender rushed over and struggled to pick up the box. "Thanks, man," he said to Simon. He nodded.

"What's going on? Why are you coming out of here?" Simon demanded.

"I dropped by to see you, but you were not here."

He cleared his throat and stepped back. "Now, you don't need to be hanging around a place like this alone."

"Simon, I came to see you."

"Well, you shouldn't be in here. This ain't no place for a lady."

I heard him, and rolled my eyes at the same time. I couldn't believe he was trying to make me feel bad for being in the club. After all, he loved to hang in there.

"I am on the way home."

"I will walk with you," he said, looking back at the club as we started to walk down the street.

"Where were you?"

"I ran downtown to pick up some things for the owner."

"The owner..."

"Yeah."

"I must have missed him because I didn't see him inside."

"I met him downtown."

Simon was lying as if it was nothing. There was not an expression of guilt on his face. And I doubt it if he'd come from downtown. I no longer knew him; the lies were becoming more and more frequent.

"Where are the supplies?"

"They are in the vehicle. I couldn't lift but one box at a time."

"I was about to ask you about the car. Where is it?"

"It is behind the club."

"Well, why don't you drive me home?"

"It is such a nice day today, I thought it would be nice to walk you home, like I used to do in Jefferson County," he said, smiling.

I agreed with him. The temperature was mild, and the sun was shining bright. It was the perfect day for a walk around the neighborhood, which was filled with scenery. It had every colored business imaginable. It even had an old colored cobbler who made shoes just for coloreds. Folks said it would cost an arm and a leg even though he got the leather cheap from a farmer he knew. I had left home to walk and clear my head and now I was more confused than ever.

"I suppose you will be going back to the club."

"I've got to unload my car."

"What is in the car?"

"Just some alcohol for the bar..."

We walked down the street hand in hand. For a brief moment, I thought back to the days when I first moved to Richmond and remembered how Simon, Robert and I used to stroll down the cobblestone sidewalk to take in the views. And even before Robert, Simon would wait for me on the playground under the tree, and then walk home with me. It was those memories I held close to my heart. In Richmond, we would admire the beautiful shrubbery and immaculate landscape and the well-built architecture of the Jackson Heights neighborhood. Now he was escorting me home and I knew it was only to keep me from knowing what he really had stored in his Model T. The closer we got to our house, the more curious I became.

CHAPTER 11

Momma was leaning across the balustrade observing us as we walked down the street. The brisk wind was waving her coattail back and forth as Robert held tightly on to her dress as if he was going to fall. When Simon kissed me softly on the lips and turned to walk back up the street to the club, I could hear Momma grunting even before I placed a foot on the step leading up to my porch. It was at that moment I wanted to take two steps backward, turn around and follow Simon back to where we'd just come from. Instead, I went inside our duplex apartment anticipating Momma's comments, and as I envisioned, she followed close behind me literally kicking my heels.

"Where is Simon going?" she asked, putting Robert down to roam around on the kitchen floor.

"I'm not sure. He left his car up the street parked on the side of the club."

She listened intently, and her eyes appeared like tiny slits as if she was in disbelief of what I was saying. "It is chilly out there. I was wondering where Simon left his vehicle—seem to me he would have driven you home like most decent men." She glanced toward the window. "The wind is stirring mighty fierce out there." Outside, the trees were leaning and the March wind was pushing the leaves up the street.

I could tell by the tone of her voice, Momma was annoyed. I was upset too.

"I left something at the store. I'll be right back," I said, without sitting, as I pulled my scarf back up over my head.

"I saw how your eyes followed Simon when he turned to walk back up the road. I also saw the disappointment in your eyes. You're going up there to find out what is really going on with yo' husband. You didn't leave anything at the store, girl! You don't fool me," she said with her hands on her hips.

"I forgot something, Momma, I did," I said, deliberately avoiding eye contact.

She stood grounded with a scowl on her face and wrinkles in her forehead. "You got yo' mind somewhere else besides the store. Now you don't need to run after no man. Just sit on down and rest yourself. He will be home directly; no need to look for trouble." And then she sat down.

"But, Momma, I need to run out for a minute," I said, as fidgety as a drunk.

"Now, why are you acting like you desperate? If that man is doing something he don't want you to know about, then going back to the club is only going to make you mad."

I crossed my arms across my chest and began to pace the floor. "I want to see what is going on, Momma. I need to know." I tried to persuade her.

"Once you find out, what are you going to do?"

"I don't know. I just need to know."

Momma threw her hands up. "Go on, Chile."

I hesitated before I took a step. I inhaled and thought about what Momma was saying. I walked out of the kitchen and went into the bedroom. Robert crawled behind me. I picked him up and stood in front of the sitting room window staring across the street at the house Nadine lived in. My attempts to keep from going back to the club did not stick with me. I went back into the kitchen and handed Robert to Momma, who was sitting at the kitchen table. When I opened the door, Momma shook her head.

I didn't say anything; I just trotted through the trees and out of sight. I was on a mission, no matter what I might find. If I had stayed home, I would have felt miserable.

Twice, I decided to turn around—once when I passed the corner store and again when I recalled Momma's questions. I even stood in place and let the wind braze my skin pondering over my determination to catch my husband in the lie I wanted so much to avoid.

On the way up the street, I passed the same twins I'd seen downtown. They were walking in unison—with each step, their heels playing a perfect harmony of beats. It was at that moment that I remembered Kindred, and how he was also at the club. I convinced myself he had better not come my way. As the twins marched down the street and around the corner, I realized it was impossible for me to distinguish their appearance even close up. With each step they took, it reminded me of Kindred and how he was the exact duplicate of his brother. For a brief second, I allowed my mind to stay fixated on Kindred who also had been at the club salivating over Ms. Pearl, grinning just like his brother had done.

I stopped at the corner store when I noticed Simon's car drifting down the street. I stooped down behind a Studebaker and watched him cruise past me without noticing. Nadine was sitting in the front seat. My blood started to boil, and I broke out in a sweat. I had to dab my nose with my hanky. "Why was she in his car?" I mumbled. Simon pulled over on the side of the street and Nadine got out along with her children. Nadine's daughter ran around to the driver's side and Simon handed her a fistful of greenbacks. She gave it to her mother, who smiled shyly. I wanted to run up on them, but instead, I peeked from behind some stranger's car.

Simon sped up after he had dropped them off a block away from the house. I got up and followed Nadine into the store.

"Hey!" she said, shocked, studying me like any guilty person would.

I started to pull her ponytail, but something stopped me.

"What's wrong with you?" she asked.

"You've got a nerve," I blurted out, without thinking.

"What are you talking about?"

"You know what you've done."

"I haven't done anything to you," she answered, pulling her children by their hands as if they were being violated. They stared at me hard, but didn't say a word.

"You were in the car with my husband."

Her eyes grew big. "I've known Simon a long time, longer than you will ever know."

"What are you talking about?"

"We've known each other for years."

"He hasn't been in this town for years."

"We met when we were no older than my daughter, who is eight years old."

"You are probably telling a lie. I've never seen you in my town. Simon comes from around my way."

"I know that. His grandma used to live down the road from me. We spent the summers playing together until…"

"Until what?"

"I don't have to tell you nothing."

"Even if you do know him, remember he is my husband now."

The store owner walked over to us. "Now you ladies need to lower your voices. I have a business to run."

"You should tell her to leave," I said.

"I have just as much right to shop here as you do."

"Nadine, I tell you what; I will wait for you outside. I will not be disrespecting this business."

"You followed me in here."

"Like I said, I will see you outside." I walked off.

Nadine took her time coming out of the store. Her children would come to the door, peek out at me and go back inside. I knew they were looking to see if I was still waiting for her. I was waiting, propped up against an oak tree, determined not move. When she finally walked out of the store, she saw me and immediately a scowl took over her face. I came up to her. She smacked her lips. "You should have gone on home. I don't have anything to say to you."

I hesitated, because I really didn't want to do it, but inner rage was giving me more courage than I had ever had before. I was not a fighter, yet I wanted to pull Nadine to the ground and give her a whipping myself. "I want to know why you are always around my husband. Don't you have a man of your own?" I sounded like the desperate women Momma had warned me about.

Nadine kept walking as if I had not said a word. Her children stared at me like they were going to jump on me. Her youngest daughter even maneuvered her way into the conversation. "Leave my momma alone," she said. I ignored her, and then she said, "You just mad 'cause my..."

Nadine stopped her in mid-sentence and put her hand over her mouth. "Because I was in the car with Simon," she said.

I couldn't believe my ears. Nadine was determined not to answer my question, and by the way she was acting, she had a lot to hide.

I grabbed her shoulder. "Why were you in the car with Simon?" I asked. Her daughter started to say something and Nadine warned her again to hush.

"He was giving us a ride," she said, huffing and puffing from walking fast and trying to avoid me.

"Nadine, stay out of my husband's car. He is a married man!" I warned her.

She didn't say anything, but when she got close to her house, she turned to look at me and said, "I can't promise you that."

I started toward her, and stopped. My chest was heaving. I wanted to grab her, and perhaps torture her into telling me the truth, but her children were standing beside her and guarding her with all their tiny might, waiting for me to touch their mother. One of them even had his fist balled up. I looked down and my fists were balled up too.

The lady in me turned away and went up the stairs to my apartment, stomping all the way. Momma had been sitting and peering out the window at us, her face contorted with a frown from ear to ear.

"I saw everything from the window. You were outside acting like one of those women around the way, arguing about Simon. You were all up in Nadine's face, and he just ain't worth it. I told you to act like a lady and ignore all this mess. But, being in the city has changed you and I just don't know you anymore."

"I am curious, Momma. I'm learning how to finally take care of myself. Don't you think I need to know why this woman is always around my husband? You even talk about her."

"Just watch yourself. Ain't nobody perfect. Simon is a man."

It was her attitude that had me worried when I'd left Jefferson County. Coping for her was ignoring things and pretending as if everything was good. I had been the same way before I was ever pregnant with Robert. I tried to forget things were happening to me, and it only brought with it grief. Now, I was going to take care of myself.

I took Momma's advice and waited for Simon to return home. It seemed time was standing still, it took him so long. And just as I was about to turn in for the night, he showed up with a story only he would have the audacity to tell.

"Where have you been?" I asked him as he climbed in the bed.

"I told you I had things to do at the club."

"What things?" I asked.

"I was making sure everybody up there had all of their needs met."

"I guess being home is not important to you anymore."

"Carrie, I'm tired; can we talk in the morning?"

I sat up in the bed. "No, I want to know why Nadine was in your car."

"Nadine was not in my car. Who told you that lie?" he said with his head propped up on a pillow.

All of a sudden, I felt an uncontrollable urge to slap him. I reached over and backslapped him on the head so hard I could hear the hit. It was the same way my teacher, Mrs. Miller, used to do to students who could not answer her questions.

"I saw you with her!" I said, raising my voice.

Simon sat up in the bed. He had a strange look on his face. It was my first time witnessing him without words. He put his hand on his head. "I gave her a ride, and that's all," he said, stuttering.

I tried to keep my voice down since Momma was in the next room. And I knew she would be listening. She had not missed anything since she'd come for her long visit.

"You seem to have a lot of things going on lately. You walked me home to keep from letting on that Nadine was in your car. Afterwards, you lied to me. What are you really up to? You are not the boy I knew back in Jefferson."

"You act as if I don't love you. Don't I provide for you and Robert?" he said, still holding his head as if he expected to get popped again.

"You are turning things around. Why are Nadine and her children so special to you?"

"Nadine don't mean nothing to me. She is just our neighbor."

"If that is true, why didn't you say she was in your car? Why did you have to lie?"

"I don't know."

"You don't know because you are not telling the truth."

"Nadine don't mean a damn thing to me. She is just a woman across the street."

I shook my head knowing one lie can lead to many, especially if you have something to hide. I knew because I'd lied many times to Momma when I was sneaking behind her back with Simon. I guess the same thing was bound to happen to me.

CHAPTER 12

The Atlantic Coastline train was parked at the depot when we arrived. Standing in front of the colored-only section car was a rough-looking porter as black as coal. I had never seen a colored man that dark, and above all, he was beautiful. All of his features appeared to be structured perfectly on his face; his nose, mouth and eyes blended well. He was someone new, and he didn't even glance our way as Nadine's old man had done each time we arrived. I couldn't keep my eyes off of him, because he reminded me of my papa, whose skin was almost as dark. Just the day before, I had walked the same route with my momma to the depot carrying her bags, while she wore my ears out warning me about my once perfect husband. She mumbled, "You can't be too sure about love; it will fool you e'rytime." I listened intently, realizing she was not the same lady who had raised me in rural Jefferson County. Losing Herman Camm had awakened some kind of spark in her. Now she was giving me the kind of advice I wanted from her when I was young. "No woman should love no man more than she loves herself," she warned. Then she informed me of her desire to get away from me. She said my emotions toward Simon were too painful to watch.

"I've got to go home and see about my family and the farm. I suppose Carl is worried about me too by now. I was going to stay a little while longer but yo' ways are too much for me," Momma said, shaking her head, "and you running after Simon like he is the only man on God's great earth is just too much."

Having Momma around had rattled my nerves. She didn't understand me. Love seemed to have always been a struggle for her. I'd remember how when Papa would try to hug or kiss her, she would shun his friendly advances and push him away. When she was around Mr. Camm, things were the opposite. Even when he'd come home with the stench of women and liquor on him, making everyone gag, she'd still embrace him with a hug. The way she loved continued to be a mystery to me. But she was a good babysitter, and very protective of Robert. Before she came, it was difficult to get him to sleep. He sort of fell asleep from exhaustion. Now, he was on a rigorous schedule. He ate at the same time every day, and having her around had given me the freedom I longed for ever since Robert was born. I had my freedom back, and I was a child again, like I had been before mysterious Herman Camm had made his unwanted appearance.

Robert loved Momma, although at night, he whined for MeMe, his nickname for Mrs. Hall. Momma hated it when he did that. "She is a white woman. What does she know about raising a colored chile?" she had blurted out. Color never bothered me; I think Momma's real problem was jealousy. Perhaps it was because Mrs. Hall had him spoiled, and Robert and I had grown attached to her. I enjoyed talking to her about my life. Her wisdom always made sense. And, after talking to her, I'd leave feeling like I could conquer whatever was going on.

Despite the frustration Momma seemed to have with me, I knew she'd be coming back real soon. She was fascinated by the closeness of our neighborhood. Day after day, she would sit in the kitchen window, her eyes smiling with fascination at the children playing and the ladies and gents strolling down the street.

Now I was on my way back to school. As we stood waiting, I glanced around the train depot searching for Nadine's old man to suddenly appear, but he was not on the train, and I couldn't resist smiling. It was a pleasure that Nadine's man was not working. I was tired of him reminding me of the things I was already aware of. Of course, I was a married woman. None of it was any of his business anyway. He didn't even know me. Besides, he could use some help keeping Nadine under control.

Before Adam decided to come with me to the train depot, I had stopped by his house to tell him goodbye, only to find him sitting in his bedroom at his desk writing a letter to a friend he had met in school. When he noticed me standing in his doorway, a wide smile spread across his face. I grinned too. It felt like it had been months since I had laid eyes on him. Adam's distinguished look had turned many girls' heads, especially the ones at the normal school. He carried himself like he was special, and it was the same way he treated me. He was exceptionally calm, like he was pondering about something. He put down his pen and questioned me. "Where is your husband, Carrie?" he asked as if it meant something. I knew he didn't care much for Simon after he had jacked him up by the collar and warned him to leave me alone. I told Simon we were only friends, but Simon had to let Adam know I belonged to him. None of it had been successful in separating us. We were still friends and even Simon had softened around him. Until now, Simon had had nothing to worry about.

I sat down in the chair beside his large mahogany desk, and peeked over at him putting the finishing touches on the letter he was writing. On his desk, the books were neatly stacked in a row.

His desk was classic, built out of mahogany wood like most of the professors at the normal school. There were shelves all around his bedroom wall. It was a small room, one I barely paid any attention to the night I found myself in his arms. Adam had a thirst for learning and so did I. As he finished his writing, I browsed over the books on his desk. Most times when I was home, I never opened a book. Adam was my conscience.

In the corner beside his bed was a rugged-looking leather suitcase, with a sweater thrown over a portion of the top.

"Where are you going?" I asked, after noticing the suitcase.

"You never answered my question, Carrie," he said, sealing the envelope with paste.

"I don't know where Simon is. He wasn't home when I left, and I didn't have the time to wait for him."

"Did you tell him you were going back to school?" he asked, addressing the envelope, sealing it and laying it down.

"He knows I am leaving. I told him last night. He probably just forgot about the time."

"You should not be walking alone down to the train depot, carrying a bag as heavy as that one. He should have driven you back to school."

"I left before he came back home."

"Why did you do that? Wouldn't it been easier to wait for him to take you?"

"No, because I wanted to stop by to see you."

I said it without any hesitation, and immediately, my mind flashed back to the night before I'd left. As I lay in bed thinking about my husband and how disappointing he'd been to me, Simon crawled on top of me. "I'm tired," I had said to him and coaxed him off of me and turned over, but he was persistent.

"I just want to make love to you."

All I could think about was him riding down the street with Nadine in his car. "I just can't," I'd declared. But, Simon would not take no for an answer. He rubbed my back with his fingertips until I turned to face him. Then he kissed me on the neck and as usual, a warm chill traveled throughout my limbs. I released my muscles and gave in to him. Simon started by stroking my body from head to toe with his hands. And after my defenses had begun to dissolve, he glided his long tongue over my face and then from my chest to my thighs, I could feel the moisture pouring out of me. I put the back of my hand on my forehead to wipe the sweat off my face. When he entered me and began to thrust, I almost lost myself. With each rotation of my hips, I had replaced the thoughts of Simon with those of Adam. I had struggled to keep from calling out his name. Perhaps it was my anger that made me do it. I couldn't get over Simon driving Nadine around town, and the audacity of him lying to me. The thought of Adam making love to me was a whole lot easier to handle, so I moved my hips as if I was feeling the heat from Adam.

This morning, I had left home before Simon returned. I didn't want him to take me to school. It sounds strange since nobody in a good mind would choose a train with strangers over that of an automobile. I wanted to see Adam. The trust I had for Simon was diminishing slowly. And seemingly, he was being replaced.

"I'm glad you came by. I was expecting you."

"Expecting me?" I commented as if I was surprised. We both were like magnets and could not stay apart.

"I figured it was time for you to go back to school and if you hadn't stopped by, I would have dropped by the boardinghouse for a visit."

"I don't understand why you put up with me."

He smiled. "Because you need me."

He was right. I did need him. I had thought when Hester moved back to Richmond, I would stop thinking about Adam. But all I seemed to do these days was remember the kind things he had done for me. I was embarrassed by my feelings, and now I was losing control and couldn't help letting him know just how I felt.

Adam took my hand and we sat down on his bed. He started running his fingers inside my hand and a chill swept over my body. Adam began to kiss me. It was nice, more special than any before. I opened my mouth and allowed him to put his tongue deep inside. It made me tremble. He carefully lowered me down on the bed. He unlatched the hook on my dress, and pulled down my stockings. It was as if everything was in slow motion. After I was naked and holding my arms over my breasts, he started to undress. He stripped all the way down to his natural skin. He let his large shaft stand out and salute me as if I was in charge. I saw him differently all of a sudden. I forgot about his intelligence and concentrated on the sensations he was creating for me. He stroked my body tenderly with his hands and tongue. I kissed his neck and licked his ears. He smiled. I was without words. He said, "I am the man you want. I am the man you need." I inhaled and absorbed it all. I was being played a symphony of music. I moaned and even shouted with each movement. His breath was short and sharp. He talked me through it all saying, "I love you." It was so beautiful. When he decided to enter me, I was begging for him. I was dripping with moisture and slippery as if it had rained. We both were in another place, and we moaned and sang together a harmony of sighs. It was magic. When it was over, I wanted it again. Adam held me in his arms until he was ready again and we started all over.

I had lost myself. After it was over, the shadow of guilt came over me, fast stealing the memory of the best moment I had experienced with a man. "We shouldn't have," I said.

"We did what comes naturally between a man and a woman."

"Adam, it was wrong."

Then he started to ask me these stupid questions like, "Did you enjoy it?"

I answered, "Yes."

"You are my soulmate. You don't love Simon anyway," he insisted.

I sat up in the bed. "I thought I did," I mumbled.

"You should not feel bad about us. Your husband is doing whatever he wants."

"But don't all men?"

"Yes, most of the time. But, you are different. You are going to school and you are going to get the education you've desired. No man can do whatever he wants to you."

The guilt continued to haunt me. I got up, put on my clothes and went into the bathroom down the hall which was shared by everyone. I washed up and stared at myself in the mirror. I saw a girl without a smile, and one who had grown up way too fast, one who was now a floozy. I wanted to cry, but couldn't. Simon had been lying to me too, I thought.

When I picked up my things to leave, Adam did the same. "I'm going with you," he said. "I am due a trip to see my family." I smiled. I didn't try to stop him from going; I was used to him riding to school with me. We sat shoulder to shoulder on the train, like a married couple. Every time I glanced over at Adam, a smile took over his face. I grinned back even though I was nervous about what I was doing. Simon could be somewhere lurking around, I thought. Even feeling that way, I knew I was too young not to be happy. I had left a note for Simon on the kitchen table. Hopefully, he would not try to come visit me. He was probably with Nadine by now anyhow.

We made it to Petersburg way before the sun slid beneath the clouds. Adam and I spent the entire afternoon together. He escorted me to the administration building to talk to the sorority lady who had encouraged me with her stories about women and the suffrage we had experienced at the hands of our men who were supposed to love us. Mrs. Middleton said education was the only hope we would ever have to make things right for women and coloreds alike. I liked how she inspired us girls to seek for more. "You are going to make it," Adam assured me, "I didn't think I could do it at first, either, but now that I am almost done, I can get on with my life."

"What do you mean by getting on with your life? Are you going to leave Virginia?"

"I'm not sure what I will do yet. But, I heard there are plenty of places to work up north."

"I'm sure you can find something around here," I said, trying to convince him to stay.

"I might. I might even open up my own business. Ms. Maggie Walker, our community colored banker, said she would give me a loan, if only I knew what I wanted to do."

Hearing Adam talk about leaving bothered me. I found myself cringing at the thought. It felt like all the people I knew or who cared about me were leaving or were already gone. Papa had died, and I knew deep inside my heart that he loved me more than his own flesh and blood, even though he was my stepfather. He was the person I felt loved me the most, even though no one could beat Jesus Christ loving me. At least that is what they say; yet Papa came awfully close.

Adam was the only friend I had aside from Hester in Richmond. I had known from the very first time I was in Mrs. Miller's classroom. We always sat together and even competed for the best grades in class. Hester was probably the best-looking, but I was certainly the smartest. Simon soon became my best friend and lover. He was the nicest man I knew, before Nadine showed up. Now, all I desired was an education and to be able to come home to a family of love and care. It was an eerie feeling knowing my husband was home from the road, and yet it felt like he was far away. We were growing apart, and with each lie he told, he was shoving me right into Adam's arms. I was embarrassed by my ways.

Adam and I sat on the davenport peering across at each other, gazing in each other's eyes, and not knowing what to say. The attraction was intense. We were surrounded by books. Miriam was also in the parlor, her suspicious dark eyes darting back and forth from my face to Adam's. She had come downstairs and opened the front door for a visitor. But instead of going back up the stairs to our room, she'd chosen to stay. Now she was sitting in the parlor with us, watching over us like a nanny. She'd grabbed a book from the shelf, and opened it to read. However, it was wide open on her lap upside down, so we knew there was no way she was reading it. Every few minutes, she'd glance up at us like a hawk watches its prey. After a few minutes of pretending to read, she began to talk.

"Carrie, we have all the same classes this term."

"I know," I said. Most of the girls in the house took the same classes, and studied together. We all had a thirst for teaching, one of the career choices for progressive women. Many of us anticipated being accepted in society as educators for coloreds, which seemed to be our only hope for a break. Nobody wanted to die like Papa had from the sun and the hard work in the fields. His death still brought sadness to me. Just the thoughts of my papa lying in a wooden box made my eyes well up.

"So, Adam, are you going to school down here now?"

"No, why do you ask?" he said, realizing more questions were to come. He scratched his head and waited.

"Well, I see you here visiting Carrie even more than her own husband."

I dropped my head. I felt embarrassed by the audacity of Miriam. Even though what she said was true, it was none of her business. I gawked at her and rolled my eyes.

"Carrie is a good friend. I thought it would be all right to visit her since she doesn't know many people around. Is that all right?"

"We all could use a little company from time to time, I suppose."

I listened to Miriam quiz Adam as if his visits were something she needed to research. She asked him where he was from, and how many siblings he had. After a while, I cleared my throat to get her attention. She didn't hear me at first, so I did it again, only louder. She peered over at me.

"We are all here now, so let's enjoy this evening. Classes will resume tomorrow and we will not have time for anything other than studying."

A smile came across her face. "Adam, I sure wish I had a friend like you," Miriam said in a coy way.

"I'm *your* friend too, Miriam. I'll drop by to see you, too, from time to time," Adam assured her.

Miriam seemed to relax. She sat back in the chair and a permanent grin lingered on her face. It wasn't long before all three of us were talking about school and how we could not wait to graduate and begin our new journey. I smiled knowing inside the crush Miriam had on Adam. She was lonely, and needed someone too.

She had become my closest friend away from home. She was very understanding, and relished the vision she had of marriage. She had once told me, "I'm going to have at least three children. We are going to live near the city, yet far enough away to have a garden and raise pigs."

When I walked Adam to the door, I whispered in his ear, "Can you ask your cousin to stop by and check in on Miriam from time to time?"

Adam shook his head no. "Why? Because you don't want to share?" He chuckled.

I didn't answer him. This was the second time Miriam had questioned us about our friendship, and anything she imagined could have been true. I had to decide what I was going to do. I had no doubts about one thing; I had no intention of sharing Adam with Miriam.

After Adam left, Miriam and I went upstairs to our room. We talked about everything except Adam and Simon. All of a sudden, we had a million things to catch up on.

CHAPTER 13

Simon never bothered to visit me at school. When I arrived home after being away for several weeks, I had mixed feelings. I missed Simon and his courteous ways, yet Adam was quickly giving me reasons to think about him. I had been thinking about being with him again, and no matter how hard I tried, I could not forget about the day I found myself unclothed in his arms.

The first thing I did after getting home was to go and get Robert. The house was empty. There were no signs Simon had been there. On my way home, while walking past the club, I had purposely searched for his car, but it was nowhere in sight. It was not at the club, which was always his excuse whenever he was away in the evenings. I was beginning to believe he had another family somewhere on the other side of town.

Mrs. Hall was sitting in her parlor reading a book, allowing Robert to walk around as if he owned her house. He was coasting himself from chair to chair and then picking up things on the table and throwing them down. I wondered if she ever had to spank his hands.

Robert saw me and a wide grin spread across his little face, revealing the two teeth he had on the bottom. "Was he good?" I asked Mrs. Hall.

"He is always a good boy," she said, gazing at him smiling, and he peeking back at her grinning.

I waited for Robert to run over to me, but all he did was grin before he sat down and started playing with his wooden blocks.

"Robert, come here and give Momma a kiss," I said to him. Robert did not move. I went over to him, grabbed him up off the floor and kissed his plump little cheeks. He struggled for me to put him down and he sat right back down and started playing with the blocks again. It sort of bothered me. I remembered what Adam had said: "He is too young to remember you being gone."

"Mrs. Hall, how long has Robert been down here with you?" She hesitated. "Would you say, you've been gone three weeks?"

"Yes, Ma'am."

"The baby has been down here with us for over two weeks. He ain't no trouble, though."

"Do you have any idea where Simon might be?"

"Carrie, Simon is back on the road. He said he had a few cities close by he needed to go to and the entire league was excited to finally get a chance to play with the real professionals. I believe he was going to be coming to Petersburg soon as well. He said he would drop in to see you when he came through there."

"Mrs. Hall, Simon and I are not the same anymore," I said, sitting down in the wooden rocking chair across from the davenport.

"You want something to eat?" she asked and walked off toward the kitchen. Robert threw down his blocks and took off right behind her. He took a few steps, sat down and started to crawl. I walked behind him.

"I'm not that hungry."

"It is time for my husband and Robert to have their meal. We can talk in here."

Mr. Hall did the majority of the cooking because Mrs. Hall was not the best cook. It was one of those things Mr. Hall would whisper in your ear whenever she'd offer to cook. "I've got it,

Dear; have a seat," he'd say.

Mr. Hall was not a big talker, yet he always had a smile on his face. He smiled as we took a seat around the dinner table.

"Now, I didn't cook much this evening. I had some beef and vegetables, so I made a stew," Mr. Hall said.

"He makes the best stew around," Mrs. Hall added, taking a pan of cornbread out of the oven. She cut the cornbread into hefty slices, and pulled butter and milk out of the icebox and put them on the table. I got up from the table, washed my hands, and helped her fill the bowls with stew. Mrs. Hall crumbled cornbread up in Robert's plate and lifted him high on a pillow so he could feed himself. It amazed me how much she was teaching him. He waited until Mr. Hall blessed the food, before he picked up a spoon and attempted to feed himself. I was amazed by his independence.

"Robert is eating his food like a big boy," said Mr. Hall, giggling.

Mrs. Hall smiled. "He mimics Mr. Hall. You would think he was really our own flesh and blood."

"You know what they say...you feed 'em long enough, they start to look like you," Mr. Hall commented.

"I am so sorry," I said.

"What are you sorry about?" Mrs. Hall asked.

"I leave him with you all the time. Sometimes I don't even bring food to feed him."

"Robert is the joy of our lives. We love him being here," she said.

"To be honest, I hate it when you come home. We miss him so much," Mr. Hall said.

Robert was filling his mouth with cornbread and meat. He appeared to be happy. He was doing all the things I had wanted to teach him. He was even learning to use a spoon.

"I like coming down here too."

"We know you do," Mrs. Hall commented.

"Having family around is very important. We love it when you all are here. I just wish Simon was around more," Mr. Hall said.

"I wish he was around too. It seems like me going to school is pulling us apart."

"In these times, women and men need an education," Mrs. Hall quickly said.

"I think the household is much happier when both parents are around. I think a woman ought to be home taking care of the house," Mr. Hall said.

"It is the 1920s and women need to work too," Mrs. Hall countered.

"Well, teaching is a good thing for women, but these days, women want to work in the fields beside the men. Most of them can outwork a man, and are almost as strong. I still think it is better for them to be at home."

"Carrie, now don't listen to him. You get your education and things will start to change. Remember, a few years ago, a lot of women, colored and white, walked together in Washington for better treatment. It was a movement for women to be treated fairly."

"I think all women should be treated like queens. I don't want to sound unappreciative. The missus knows I adore her," Mr. Hall said.

Mrs. Hall peered across the table at him and smiled. I could see the twinkle in their eyes. He grinned.

"I am enjoying the conversation," I got out in between bites of cornbread and the best stew I had ever tasted. "Mr. Hall, is it wrong for a married man to ride around another woman's children without considering his own family?"

"No, not if the mother has given permission or if they are his own children."

Mrs. Hall cut her eyes over at him as if to quiet him.

"What's wrong?" I asked.

"Nothing is wrong," Mrs. Hall answered for the both of them.

Robert gobbled up every last bit of food on his plate. Mrs. Hall added a little more, and said, "You need to grow, little boy."

When she talked, he smiled and when she spoke, he gave her his full attention. It was so warm at the Halls' table. They seemed to share the same concerns and had the same amount of respect for each other. It took me back to a time when my papa was living. He always made us children feel special, and it was dinnertime we all looked forward to.

"You know, one day, if you don't mind, we'd like to take Robert with us to Washington, D.C. We've got some relatives up there," Mrs. Hall said.

"Kinfolk, darling; that's what we call them," he said.

"My husband's aunt and cousins live up there and it has been a while since we've visited. His aunt is old and feeble," Mrs. Hall said.

"Robert loves it here. You are our family," I said.

Mr. Hall got up from the table and walked away, wiping his brow with a handkerchief.

"You all right, Mr. Hall?" I asked.

"You and Robert are like the family we never had," said Mrs. Hall. "He is just happy."

Mrs. Hall put Robert on the floor and he ran into the parlor behind Mr. Hall.

"Mrs. Hall, I feel my marriage is about over," I said, once we were alone.

"Is it because of your feelings for Adam?"

"I don't think so. Adam is the best friend any girl could have. He is always there for me and in places I wish my husband could be."

"Marriage should be centered on love. Do you love Simon?"

"Yes, Ma'am, I think I do."

"If you are still in love with Simon, don't go leading Adam on. He will never forgive you for that."

"Mrs. Hall, maybe I'm falling out of love. Every time my husband and I are together, Nadine manages to come for a visit. Simon even had Nadine and her children in his car."

"Well, there is nothing wrong with giving somebody a ride."

"He's been seen with her in Petersburg. The girls at the house told me about it."

"They lie, too, young lady."

"I know, but Adam saw him the same weekend in Petersburg."

"Child, I feel sorry for you. You don't know which way to turn."

"I don't, Mrs. Hall. I don't."

"Can I make a suggestion?"

"Yes, Ma'am."

"If Simon will not give you the truth, talk to Nadine. She is bound to come clean at some point."

"I tried to talk to her and she just kept on walking."

"Maybe you should try again. Walk across the street, and knock on her door."

"I'm sort of scared. I really think she is more to Simon than a friend. I have caught her in my house before and now they are spending time together in Petersburg. Mrs. Hall, he's never around when I'm ready to go back to school. I feel he doesn't care anymore."

"You left without him even knowing last time."

"Did he tell you that?"

"Of course he did. He asked me why you left without saying anything."

"I left a note."

"Why didn't you tell him?"

I hesitated before I answered her. She kept peering over at me with those icy-blue eyes and I finally broke my silence. "I wanted to see Adam."

"Did Adam go to school with you?"

"Yes, Ma'am, he did."

"I think he is the one you've chosen to be with."

"I trust him; he has always told me the truth."

"You need to find out what your husband's attraction to Nadine is. Then you need to be honest with yourself and Adam. He deserves the truth."

As I listened to her speak, I realized my life had become more complicated with each year of living. With the move to Richmond, I had expected to be free of all the baggage and fear.

CHAPTER 14

Ms. Pearl was known in Virginia, Maryland, Washington, D.C., and even North Carolina. As I walked down the road to school every day, I'd walk past places where posters with her picture on it were placed in the front window. It was very persuasive. She was the toast of the town. Many of the people from Petersburg gathered at the train depot on Friday evenings anxious to go to Richmond. They wanted to hear Pearl Brown and to see her "rotate her hips," one man standing at the depot said, imitating how she moved. Miriam had asked me several times about her. "Is she as pretty as folks say?" My answer to her was yes.

Ms. Pearl was a beautiful lady and she knew it. When she walked, she threw her full bosom out, kept her back straight as an arrow and strutted across the floor. She had the kind of confidence many of us young women wanted. When people talked about her, she didn't seem to mind. She would walk right past gossiping women and slyly smile. She appeared to live by her own standards, and not those of the people whispering behind her back.

Chatter was all around me. I could hear voices behind me talking about Ms. Pearl's new man.

"How can she fool around with Kindred Camm? He is Herman's brother," one of the ladies riding the train home to Richmond said.

The lady riding beside her turned up her nose. "That woman is just a country floozy. She has probably been with every man in this town. People think she can sing. She can't sing, either."

"Now, Rosa, she can sing. She has got herself a good voice. I disagree with that."

"Like I said, she is a slut," I heard her say, as if it was a truth declared and signed off on.

"I'm going to see her perform," the lady said.

"She can't sing, I tell you. You are going to be wasting your hard-earned dollars."

"I'm going to see her and I want you to go with me."

"I ain't going to see her sing. She ain't like Bessie and Maggie. Now *they* can sing."

"Rosa, you have never heard her sing. You need to stop gossiping about folks and come and see for yourself."

"I might go while I'm up here."

Ms. Pearl had people talking everywhere. Not all of the talk was positive. It was mainly about her love affairs and almost never her singing. Listening to these women talk was the first time I had ever heard of her singing described as bad. She was the best singer I had ever heard, and most people would agree. The boisterous ladies swore right out that Kindred Camm was her new man and one of them said, "I sure hope that white man don't find out; he just might kill him like he did poor Willie."

When I heard them speak of Willie, my mouth flew wide open, and a chill traveled throughout my body. Simon and I had been at the club that night. We'd witnessed the entire thing. The white man was the killer, and he was still walking around like a peacock, as if he owned the club and Ms. Pearl.

The ride home was shaky. The train appeared extra crowded.

It was the first of the month and the soldiers and a lot of the workers had just gotten paid. All of them were ready to live it up in the big city of Richmond.

Once the train stopped in Richmond, the people scattered in various directions. I skipped right past Adam's place and headed down Broad Street toward Jackson Heights. The closer I got to the club, which had not opened yet for business, the more anxious I became about looking in on Ms. Pearl. When I turned the corner leading to Jackson Heights with my suitcase in my hand, I noticed Simon's car parked on the corner beside the club.

I convinced myself Nadine was somewhere close by. I turned the knob on the club door, and it was unlocked. I opened the door and walked in. The bartender noticed me and said, "We are not open yet, Ma'am."

"I know," I responded. "I came to see Simon."

"I remember you," he said. "Simon's in the back with Ms. Pearl." He signaled with his head in the direction of the back room. I smiled and thanked him. Ms. Pearl was always in that room. It was her dressing room, yet I could sense a lot of other things happened there. I paused before knocking on the door, inhaled and then proceeded to tap lightly. I could hear stirring from the other side of the door. I patiently waited for someone to open up. The white man cracked opened the door and peered out at me. "What do you need?" he asked, in a deep baritone voice.

"I want to see Simon, please," I said, my heart thumping hard in my chest.

He kept the door cracked and peeked around at the people in the room. "Simon, are you in here?"

I heard Simon's voice. "Yeah, let 'em in."

The white man opened the door and motioned for me to step

in. I took a deep breath; a wave of fear had swept over me like a shadow. I struggled to contain my fear of what I might witness going on inside. I stood close to the door and my eyes panned the room. Simon was leaning back on the davenport with his legs crossed. When he saw me, he immediately stood up.

"What are you doing here?" he asked, without even greeting me.

Ms. Pearl spoke. She was sitting in front of a mirror admiring her hair, patting it down and smiling. In her other hand, she held a drink. She glanced at me and smiled. "Hi, Baby, how you doing?"

"I'm okay, Ms. Pearl," I muttered. I was afraid.

"You sure?" she asked, twirling a curl in her fingers.

"Yes, Ma'am," I replied.

She glanced at me and winked subtly.

Simon rushed over to me; he then tugged me by my hand and coaxed me toward the door. I locked eyes with Ms. Pearl, and she nodded at me. I didn't dare murmur a word, but I gently smiled. Before I exited with Simon, I noticed the tall stack of greenbacks on the small table beside the davenport where he had been sitting. The room was more than a dressing room. A pistol was also on the table pointing toward the wall. And I wondered if it belonged to Simon. No telling what actually took place in the back room.

"What are you doing in here?" Simon asked as soon as we were out of the door.

"I saw your car outside."

He peered down at me with his dark, almond-shaped eyes and they appeared cold and disturbed. He didn't like me being there.

"Why are you here, Simon? Are you working?" He continued directing me out of the club.

"You shouldn't be here; this is not the place for a lady. I told you to stay out of here."

"I wanted to see you."

"Okay, but if it's not an emergency, it could have waited until I made it home," he said, coaxing me toward the front door.

"We need to talk."

"Can it wait until I get home?"

"When are you coming home?"

"I'm going to drive you home right now. This is not the place for a decent young woman."

"Why are you always here?"

He shook his head and did not answer me. He told the bartender, "Man, let Ms. Pearl know I will be right back."

"Sho will," the bartender answered as he continued to wipe the counter.

Simon picked up my bag and ushered me to the car.

"Simon, you are acting very strange."

"I don't think a girl barely eighteen ought to be in a club alone." I frowned.

"Did you hear me?" he asked, driving faster than usual.

"I heard you."

He raised his voice. "Why are you always getting into my business, Carrie? Don't I take good care of you?"

I took offense at his statement and tears welled up in my eyes.

"Now what is your problem?" he asked, as mean as he could be.

"Simon, you are not the man I used to know."

He bit his lip, then he boldly said, "And you are not the same innocent young girl I met back in Jefferson. You are hanging out in nightclubs and have forgotten about your child. You done left him with a white lady to raise."

What he said made me angry. I was breathing deeply, trying to control my temper. Simon drove past the corner store and there was Nadine walking down the sidewalk. She saw Simon and waved like an anxious child. When she noticed me in the car, she quickly turned her head and dropped her hand as if she had done something wrong. I rolled my eyes.

"I'm the same girl that wanted an education and I thought you were the same boy that wanted to play professional ball," I reminded Simon.

"You have started to act like the city girls, hanging out in places good girls don't belong."

"Are you saying I act like Nadine?"

"Nadine don't have nothing to do with us."

"Well, why is she always in your car? And when she sees you, she acts like a young girl in love."

He stopped in front of the tenement house. "Nadine is not in my car."

"You know I am truly trying to get an education and Mrs. Hall is kind enough to help me out. She and her husband watch Robert and don't ask me for anything."

Then he said it again, "You are not the same innocent little girl I first met. Now you are hanging in Petersburg and doing things your momma would have a fit about."

I inhaled, and felt the heat rise over my body. I peered across at him. He was no longer the handsome ball player and the envy of all the girls at school. He was now making annoying comments and I suspected he was also a liar.

I had to dig deep to conjure up the nerve to challenge him. "I don't care what you say about me. People say you are not who you say you are. And folks have seen you driving around Petersburg with Nadine in the car. Now how does that look?"

He shook his head, and frowned. "They are just making things up. People are always talking."

"Simon, stop. Don't lie to me!" I screamed, since he was determined to keep denying the truth.

He turned toward me and stared me in the eyes. His almond eyes appeared dark with worry. "Since when do you listen to the gossip of other people? You know people will make things up. I want you to stop asking me about Nadine or any of the other things stewing up in your head."

I opened the car door and got out. He got out too and followed me up the stairs to our apartment on the second floor, both of us planting our feet with a strong determination on the steps. We were both agitated.

After we were in the house, I informed him he was sleeping on the davenport. I went into the bedroom and threw a pillow out to him like he was a dog. The pillow almost hit him in the face, but instead, it tumbled on the floor.

"Girl, you are crazy!" he yelled, bending down to pick up the pillow. I peeked out the door a few minutes later. He was lying on the davenport with his eyes shut tight.

I didn't open my mouth. I had said enough. We both went to sleep early. Neither of us bothered to eat anything. I tossed and turned all night. He didn't go back to the club as he'd said he would.

CHAPTER 15

Hester came over to the house early one Saturday morning. The sun had just begun to ascend into the sky. She'd always been an early riser, so seeing her at that time in the morning was no surprise to me. Country folks got up with the chickens and went to bed with the sun. Simon had gotten up early too, washed, made a pot of strong coffee, dressed and was out the door before 7:30 a.m. He said he was headed to the club because he had business to take care of. The club didn't open before noon. Folks who stay up at night, often sleep most of the day. It is why Momma called them "all-night ramblers."

Hester and I decided to spend the entire day together. We started to act like we had in secondary school. We sat down at the kitchen table beside each other and discussed the men in our lives.

We started off with my brother, John, who had been dating Hester. John had been spending more time around Ms. Pearl, a woman too old for him. He claimed to be handling some legal things for her, coming down from Washington, D.C. to settle some of her business, or so Hester had said. "Ever since he helped her get out of jail, he has felt as if he was her adviser or something," I said.

"Ms. Pearl doesn't need John. He is like all the rest of the men around; they fall for her. They like the glamour and just being in her presence."

"She is too old for him, and besides, I think you are making too much of it," I told her. My brother felt he could save the world. He had always been softhearted for the derelicts and unfortunate. It seemed to work for everyone except me.

"I am just not going to stand back and let Ms. Pearl steal my man. She already has her share and more. It is the reason most of the women around can't stand her."

We both giggled, knowing it was the truth. Ms. Pearl had every man in town wishing he could be with her. She knew it, and ignored most of them. She was very selective, and catered to only a few close male friends, even though other men were praying she would give them a chance.

"What is Simon up to these days?" Hester asked between chuckles and sips of coffee. "Your Simon used to be a good man. He was different than the rest of the boys we knew," Hester said, after asking where Simon had gone so early in the morning.

"He is still different. And, he is good, but there is the side that remains a mystery to me. He has a lot of secrets."

"Is it Nadine that you worry about?"

I paused to think about her question. "Not really, even though I find myself thinking about how much I don't know about my husband. I worry more about Kindred being Mr. Camm. He is the one keeping me looking over my shoulder."

Hester squinted and peered over at me. She twisted her lips as if I had struck a nerve. I watched her facial expression change from a smile to a crease in her forehead. She was in deep thought, and she was fidgety. For some reason, she always had thoughts far beyond her years in age. Now she was quiet, adjusting herself in the chair, and just staring at me.

"What is wrong with you?" I asked, after sipping on my drink and breathing in the aroma of coffee.

She shook her head. "Aint nothing wrong with me," she said, without cracking a smile.

"What are you thinking about then?" I asked, waiting.

"Nothing at all..." she answered.

"Why are you so quiet then?"

"I don't know if I should tell you this," she said, hesitating.

"Tell me what?" I asked, and waited for her to answer me.

She finally inhaled and said, "Carrie, it seems as though Kindred is staying down in Jefferson."

"What is he doing down there? Just the other day he was hanging at the club sniffing around Ms. Pearl."

"People have been seeing him with your momma from time to time."

"My momma...now who could be making this story up?" I asked, positive it was a mistake. Folks in Jefferson County were famous for turning the truth into a lie and for making up their own stories.

"They say Mrs. Mae Lou and he were together at church the other Sunday. They came together and left together. They even sat together on the third row."

"What do you mean, at church?" I asked getting more wound up with each word flowing out of her mouth.

"They came to church together, like a couple. Momma said Mrs. Mae Lou was dressed real nice."

"Hester, my momma has sense enough to stay away from Kindred."

"Mrs. Mae Lou got the entire town talking again. She says he is Herman's brother. But now, I'm not sure."

"How do you know all of these things?" I asked, thinking what a shame it was if Hester had become a gossip like the rest of the town.

"My momma told me, and she don't have no reason to lie on your momma. She seemed to be a little worried about Mrs. Mae Lou."

"I know she wouldn't lie on her. It's just hard to believe," I said.

Why was Momma fooling around with her dead husband's brother? Herman had some kind of spell on my momma. There was a lady around Jefferson County known for working roots on people.

"You need to go home soon and find out for yourself," Hester suggested.

"There has got to be an explanation for all of this. Momma knows my fear of that man. So why is she spending her time with somebody like him."

Hester shook her head and smacked her lips at my comment. "Remember, he has not done anything. The only crime Mr. Kindred has committed is looking like his brother so far."

"I can't get used to him being around. I've never seen any twins who look that much alike. The girls that live around the corner each have something different about them. One is taller than the other or something."

"People have said there are twins that look so much alike, they are constantly mistaken for one another. It is obvious Mr. Camm and his brother was like that. Too bad Camm had such a bad reputation in the community, drinking and carrying on. And let's not forget what he did to you."

"I left Jefferson County to get away from all of the madness. Now it is following me wherever I go."

Hester was quick to shoot back, "Nobody is doing anything to you. You are doing it to yourself. You are running around afraid of somebody like Kindred, and you are putting up with Simon and his questionable ways. It is time you put a stop to them one by one."

"How do you suggest I handle things?" I asked, knowing she had thought about everything and had a plan waiting to be implemented.

"Since Kindred is on your mind the most, let's take a trip to Jefferson and just see what is up with Mrs. Mae Lou."

"I can't take Robert down to Jefferson; everybody will be talking."

"They are going to talk no matter what you do. Ginny is there and you know how glad she would be to see you and Robert," Hester said, and glanced over at me. "Let's go soon."

I hesitated to commit. I didn't want to see my momma with Kindred. And if he was visiting her, I was sure I would not stay with her.

"I haven't seen Ginny in a long time. I know she will know what is going on, and I can stay with her while we are there."

"Just let me know when and I will go with you. We can make it a fun trip."

"I probably will not have time to visit. I just want to make sure my momma is all right."

"She is happy, they say. I just wonder if he is more to her than a brother-in-law."

"I don't understand. She is not the same woman that raised me. She would never be seen with a man of his caliber. But she surprised us with Herman. What if this man is also taking advantage of her Southern hospitality?"

"Mrs. Mae Lou is a strong woman. She can handle herself in any circumstance."

"You are right." I laughed. "I can remember how she handles a rifle. I think she is a better shot than my papa and my brothers. She is a tough woman, but when it comes to men, she seems to be taken in by them."

Hester shook her head and then she said, "You know Richmond was supposed to be a new start for you. You were going to get an education and walk away from all the hurt of Jefferson County.

Now you are worried about a twin, your husband is changing, and you have a new friend in your life. I think you need to start eliminating the things causing you fear and get some control over your life."

"I thought I had it worked out. But it is not over yet. I am still worried and it bothers me more than you even know. I've got to talk to Momma first."

"You are more important than any of this stuff. Take care of your life first. You must deal with Simon. Your momma can handle herself."

I had to convince her of the mystery of Kindred. "I can't let him hurt her like he did before. Herman Camm was a cruel and selfish man. Why did he have to return?"

Hester laid her hand on my shoulder and massaged it as if to comfort me. "Remember, he is his twin. It is not Herman."

"So everyone believes," I quickly said.

"How can you prove it any other way?" she asked, staring me in the eyes.

"I don't know, but I think it is Herman," I said. I could not prove he was Herman, but I had to find a way for me to tell the difference.

"Do you realize if the folks in the country thought he was Herman, he would probably be dead and in the ground by now?" Hester commented, knowing Herman had left a lot of enemies behind, including the white man at the club, whom I believe was a real gangster type.

CHAPTER 16

I spent the evening at home with Simon. He had come home early carrying a single rose and a fried chicken dinner he had picked up at the restaurant around the corner from the club. The food was always hot, and people said it was the best soul food restaurant in town. I didn't know of but one other place that sold hot food. Simon had taken me to the restaurant several times and I loved the spicy taste of that food. The meal included two pieces of chicken, bread and potato salad. "I told them to make your chicken sandwich while I waited. I told them my wife likes her food piping hot," Simon said, smiling, a far cry from the month before when neither of us cracked a grin in the other's direction. He had been consistent, though. Each day he had been showering me with compliments and bringing home the little things he thought I enjoyed. One evening he came home with a Coca-Cola in one bag and some rose water perfume in the other. I didn't tell him I hated the scent of rose water.

It had been weeks since we had spent any quality time together. I had passed him several times in our own small apartment and we didn't part our lips. Just believing he had spent time with Nadine, my neighbor, made me sick at the stomach. Nadine was no friend of mine and I hated her being a friend to him. "Nadine don't mean nothing to me. She is just somebody I know," he'd argued whenever I mentioned her name. I'm not sure if ever I believed him.

One night, while I was alone in bed, I decided Nadine was not going to interrupt my marriage. I had to fight for what was mine, even though at times my mind would end up daydreaming about a life with Adam. What we had was also wrong. I enjoyed Adam's company more than anybody. He understood colored people were sick and tired of serving white folks. We wanted meaningful work, and were tired of working in the fields and in white folks' kitchens. Too many people had fallen to their death in the tobacco fields working in the high sun, until the white man said, "enough." At least with an education, I could help train our future business-men, doctors and educators. Colored folks could have their own businesses, and maybe colored women could do more than care for the needs of the lily white lady.

Simon had my full attention when he handed me the gifts. I quickly put the single rose in a vase of water and put the sandwich in the oven to eat later. I grinned like I had the first night he made love to me. It had been a long time. After I threw my arms around his neck, he reached down, picked me up, and carried me to the bedroom. But before he started to caress me, I excused myself into the bathroom to insert my sponge. Afterward, I felt relieved about being protected from having a child I was not ready for.

He pulled me into his long muscular arms. He gazed at me with those beautiful mahogany eyes as if he was reading my soul. He missed me, I could tell. I stared back into his eyes, and smiled shyly. I wanted him. So when he laid me down on the bed, beads of sweat had already started to surface on my nose and around my hairline. Simon kissed me long and passionately on my lips, his tongue deep inside my mouth, connecting us as one. My heartbeat was quick and my breathing was heavy. I shivered when he ran his tongue over my nipples and down my stomach. I twitched when he palmed my bottom with his hands and pulled me close to him. It was at that moment that I could not hold back and he slid right into my juices. I moved my hips up, down and around. Simon was controlled and I knew it took all the self-control he had to keep from slamming himself into me. I could feel his heartbeat. And as he moved in and out of my body, I could sense the enjoyment in his eyes. He inhaled as if he was sniffing roses. We climaxed together. Afterward, we snuggled close, I laid my head on his chest and we both fell off to sleep.

My relationship with Simon was finally reminding me of old times in Jefferson, when all I thought about was us. He was being the kind of man I had fallen in love with, and for some reason, I no longer craved the attention of Adam, yet I thought about him daily. I had not seen him in a long time, though. Everything was surprising since I expected Simon to come up with a story about needing to leave to play ball with the colored league. "Are you going out to play ball?" I asked him.

"Yes, I will always play ball. It is in my blood," he said, smiling. He walked over to the door, picked up the bat behind it and started swinging the bat like he was hitting a ball.

"I knew you couldn't do without it."

He set the bat down behind the door. "I love playing ball. It makes me happy. A man needs something to do outside of family."

I listened to the disappointment in his voice and could tell he was having a hard time being the man I wanted him to be. He was still craving the road and playing ball. And for some reason, I knew he couldn't stick to the schedule he had maintained for several weeks. He had been coming home from the club early each day. He was spending more time with Robert, picking him up from the Halls in the evening.

The night he had spent on the davenport had been an eye-opener for him. It was when he finally took me seriously. I was a young girl forced to grow up fast. I was country and naïve, but I wasn't stupid. I had said to him, "Simon, if you want to be with Nadine and tell me lies, you need to leave. I am tired of the way you have been treating me."

"I love you," he had said the next morning, after tossing and turning on the davenport and begging me to let him back into the bedroom. I was determined to stand up for myself. I told him how I felt and after days without talking, he had said he wanted to make me happy. I didn't have the nerve to tell him that I had feelings for another man. I wanted to keep Adam out of it all. I still loved Simon and I didn't want our marriage to end without even trying. So I'd told him I loved him too.

"What are we going to do?"

"I want you to be honest with me. I am afraid about how our relationship has turned out."

Simon stood listening to me and when I was done, he pledged he would not lie to me again. When I asked about Nadine being in his car, he pleaded with me to forget about Nadine. He convinced me she was just someone he had known in the past and she meant nothing to him now. He had felt sorry for her and her children and given them a ride home. I accepted his answers and for the past three weekends, we had been courteous and accountable to each other.

I knew it would be short-lived by the way he was standing in the kitchen swinging the bat as if he was prepared to bat a ball away. When he put the bat back behind the door, I could see the jovial smile disappear on his face.

"Do you miss the game?"

"No, not really," he said without looking at me.

I had been back to school twice since I found him in the club. Simon took me to school each time in his Model T. Both times, we rode right past Adam's tenement. I glanced over at the building hoping to catch a glimpse of him walking down the sidewalk. He was never in sight. It was so strange how I had my husband's attention, yet hoped to get a glimpse of Adam because I had begun to miss him.

When Simon parked the car in front of the boardinghouse on the second trip, he informed me he was headed out of town for a few days.

He patted me on the thigh. "I've got to go down south for a few days." I cringed at the thought.

I knew it was coming, and I anxiously responded, "I was expecting you to leave. I knew you couldn't stick around for a month. I just knew it."

He took my hand. "Carrie, you are not home. You are here in Petersburg most of the time."

"I know I'm here. It is just the idea of knowing you are home waiting for me."

Simon smiled. "Look, we will probably be home around the same time. I am only going for a few days."

"Is this a baseball trip?"

He tucked his chin. "Sort of."

"Where are you going then?"

"I'm not going far. I have some business to take care of and it involves baseball."

I didn't understand anything he was saying. He didn't say much and he never really gave me a direct answer.

"Simon, I sure hope everything will turn out okay."

"It will be all right. I am going to meet Pete Hill, and see if I can help him and the league in any way."

"I thought you wanted to play."

"I do, but being around the game is just as important. Well, I've got to go."

He reached over and kissed me longer than normal. It was like we had done in Jefferson County many times when he was leaving. I remembered being in the school yard kissing over and over again. We both would be breathing hard. It was a time when I was sure he had his mind on me.

There was something about the way he tucked his head and glanced away that made me nervous. I knew there was more to the trip than he had let on. I was finally realizing my husband had more things going on than anything he was willing to tell me about.

Simon got out of the car and set my suitcase inside the door of the boardinghouse.

"Are you coming inside?" I asked, still standing on the front porch where one of the tenants was sitting in a rocking chair enjoying the warmer than usual temperature.

He pulled out his pocket watch and glanced at the time. "No, I want to get back to Richmond and do a few errands before I have to leave tonight."

He kissed me one last time before he got back into the car.

I stood outside watching as he turned the vehicle around and sped off in the direction of Richmond. I knew he would be gone when I came home for the weekend.

The next morning, on the way to class, I heard a faint call from a distance. "Carrie, Carrie!"

The voice was familiar, so I turned around to see who it was. Just like I had thought, it was Adam almost trotting to catch up with me.

"Hi!" he said. "I thought it was you."

It was so nice to see him. "What are you doing down here?"

"I'm going to be working at the school. I graduated, so I'm going to be teaching a class."

"It is so strange seeing you here," I said, never believing he would be in Petersburg. "Are you living here now?" He smiled.

"No, I'm staying with my cousins during the week. I plan on going back to Richmond on the weekend. I'm thinking about buying myself a used Model T from one of the professors at the school."

"When were you going to tell me about your job?"

"I'm telling you now. I got hired last week. Everything is new to me. Besides, I haven't seen you in over a month. I thought you had forgotten about me."

I chuckled at his sarcasm. Forgetting him was not anything I wanted to do. Simon had been working on building my trust. And, it was working. Nadine was no longer a threat to me. She was just a pathetic woman seeking the attention of men. She had even made a pass at Adam. But he didn't pay her any attention.

I felt deceitful chatting with Adam after convincing myself the only man I wanted was Simon. The more I listened to Adam, the easier it became for me to forget about Simon who had just dropped me off the day before. I had pretty much led him to believe things were back to normal and even better than before. I had forgiven him for his association with Nadine and I had made passionate love to him which sealed my commitment to him, even though thoughts of Adam still flashed through my mind. Now Adam being in Petersburg could only be trouble for a married girl.

CHAPTER 17

Hester and I left for Jefferson County before the rooster out back crowed. We caught the first train of the day, which usually pulled out of the depot around 6 o'clock in the morning. There had not been any warnings we were coming. So, as we departed the train, we knew Momma, Ginny and my brother were in for a happy surprise. I relished the times when I could come home without digging up the memories of an unhappy time I longed to forget. I had some great memories there; however, the dark seemed to overshadow the light. Nothing much had changed since I had been gone. One of the people who had made me fearful of returning was Bobby, the sheriff. Bobby was always trying to keep someone locked up at that tiny jail he worked in. He was a dumb rednecked man, who, with every chance he got, threatened to lock somebody colored behind bars. He felt he was better than the colored people, but Aunt Ginny said he had drunk her breast milk many times as a baby. And when he got out of line, she held that fact above his head. John, my eager brother fresh out of law school, had forced Bobby to release Ms. Pearl from his jail. Like always, Bobby was exerting his power. He didn't have any evidence against Ms. Pearl, just a country boy hunch.

"I'm going to go on home now," Hester said, as we approached her parents' yard, after walking the quarter of a mile down the road.

"Okay," I replied, even though I had secretly wished she would go home with me.

Dirt was all over our shoes. I took out my handkerchief, and dusted the toes of my shoes off. "Why are you doing that?" Hester asked. "Your shoes are not going to stay shiny around here. All we have are dirt roads."

"I know," I answered, and continued knocking off the dust.

"Are you all right?" Hester asked.

"I'm fine."

"You sure you don't want me to go with you home?"

We were exactly three feet from the front door of her parents' house, and I could sense her momma peeping from behind the curtains.

"I really don't want to go home alone. I'm not sure I will be able to handle what I might find."

"I tell you what, if I go with you to your momma's house, you can come back home with me and stay the night."

"If Momma is alone, you can stay with me," I said, wondering if Kindred would be there.

"Well, we can't just stand here," Hester said. "Let's say hi to Momma and then keep on to your house." We knocked on the door and her mother opened it. She had a smile on her face, and she reached out to give us a hug. "Come on in; I was watching y'all from the window." She insisted on pouring us something to drink, even though we told her we were headed to my momma's house. "You still need something to kill your thirst; Mae Lou is a ways down the road." We sat at her table for almost an hour laughing and talking, with Hester's mother refilling our glasses with lemonade ever time it got low. Hester's mother loved entertaining, and she was such a good communicator, we had both almost forgotten about our destination. When we got up to leave, she reminded us she would be waiting for us when we got back.

"I want to see Ginny before I leave too. You know she can't get around like most folks," I said, as we walked down the road past the fields of tobacco and corn.

"We can check on Ginny tomorrow," Hester said, grabbing my hand as we had done as children.

Hester had been my best friend ever since we sat beside each other in the first grade. At first, we didn't talk, but after a while, we were chatting in the classroom and Mrs. Miller would have to quiet us down. We had so much in common. We liked to read, and we both were determined to forgo the career of a farmer. She had been with me through all the ups and downs and we shared everything. Whenever she was around, I'd have this sense of security. I remember begging Momma to let me stay the night with her. We'd stay up late watching the shadows on the wall from the candle flickering while we talked about boys and what our plans were for our future. Her family was very kind. Her mother always had her hair braided and wrapped in a bun, and she wore cinnamon powder even on weekdays. She worked around the house just as Momma did, yet not a hair on her head ever looked out of place. She reminded me of Mrs. Ferguson, who always wore red lipstick. At night, Hester's momma would lie across the bed with Hester and me, and we would talk about everything. When it was time to leave, I'd go home wishing my momma would talk to me.

We took our time walking down the dirt road. The sun had been up a while, yet we didn't see anybody on the empty road ahead. Long before we got close to the house, we could see smoke from the kitchen stove billowing in the air. The closer we got to the house, the more nervous I became. A chill went throughout my body. I remember thinking no one should have this much anxiety coming home. Home should be a safe place.

I knocked on the door.

Momma came to the door fully dressed with an apron around her waist. "Lord, Carrie, what are you and Hester doing down here?" she asked.

"I thought I would surprise you and pay you a visit," I said, waiting for her to ask us in.

"Surprise me? Well, this is new," she said, and opened the door. "Come on in."

The heat hit us at the door. It was hot inside, but luckily, the fireplace was dying down. We quickly took off our sweaters and hung them on the rack. The house had an aroma of bread baking in the oven.

"What were you doing, Momma? I can smell the food in the kitchen."

"Let me go in here and check on the biscuits." A grin spread across my face and Hester's too. I loved Momma's cooking. She was no doubt the best cook around. She could make anything taste good. She said her momma made her learn to cook at seven years of age. I started cooking breakfast when I was about ten; it would have been sooner, but Papa would not let me.

When Momma hurried into the kitchen to check on the bread, Hester and I followed right behind her. When we got to the door, we noticed Kindred sitting at the kitchen table. He was sitting in the same place my papa had sat as well as Kindred's brother, Herman. I cringed. It was just what I didn't want to see.

"How y'all doing?" he asked.

I gritted my teeth and braced myself. I could feel the heat overcoming my body, and an uncontrollable frown rippling across my face. I couldn't open my mouth. Hester answered for me, short but sweet. "We're fine."

Momma was quick to explain him being there. "Kindred have been staying here for a few weeks. He's been helping me around the house. Y'all knows he is Herman's brother."

All of a sudden my stomach started to turn somersaults. The eagerness to eat Momma's food was gone. I wanted to turn around and walk right back out of the door.

"Has Carl been over here today?" I asked, ignoring Kindred, who was holding a fake grin on his face. Momma was fidgety as she took the bread out of the oven and laid it on the stove.

"Carl don't come over as much as he used to. He got a whole lot of work over there to finish up. I done told him to slow down, but he is just like his papa; he can't stop working." Momma pulled out the butter.

We sat down at the kitchen table. Kindred did not move. He just sat there in Papa's chair and peered at us from on the other side of the table. He was too comfortable. He had the same dark beady eyes as Herman; he was the spitting image of his brother. It was the first time I had been so close to him, and I was very uncomfortable. I was shaking my leg uncontrollably the entire visit; it was my way of dealing with my nerves. I studied him, just like I had the twins in Richmond. His hands were long and slim like his brother's, and everything about him seemed too much the same for him to be a brother. Kindred was so much like Herman, I wanted to lash out at him.

"Where do you sleep?" I asked Kindred. But, before he could answer, Momma answered for him.

"Now you know he is over in the boys' old room. Where else would he be?"

"I just wanted to make sure my room was still vacant," I quickly added.

She turned around and gave me a hard stare. Hester held her breath and so did I. Momma turned back around and walked over to the stove. She took out some eggs, cracked them and tossed them in the fatback oil.

"Go on and put your things in your room," she directed. "Where's my grandson? I know you didn't leave him with that white lady."

"I'd like to meet my family," Kindred said, which meant he knew Herman was my baby's father.

I didn't even acknowledge his comment. Robert was my son, and he was not any family of his.

Momma mumbled, "I sure hope he don't end up thinking that white lady up yonder is his momma."

She was right. It was easy for me to leave my son because I trusted the Halls. I was glad I didn't bring him to Jefferson to be exposed to the disrespect of his grandma, and even though she said Kindred was sleeping in my brother's room, I could tell she was lying.

"The Halls are good people."

"I sort of miss my grandson; he is such a good child," Momma said, grinning.

Momma seemed different. She was taking swift steps and appeared prissy, tightening up her dress around the waist and at times glancing over at Kindred in a friendly way. It was a replay of the way she acted when Herman Camm first started coming around.

Hester had been quiet. She was observing and snacking on a biscuit with butter that Momma had set on the table. "So, Mr. Kindred, are you from around here?"

"Well, I was raised around here, but I've been gone from around here for many years now."

"What made you come back?" she asked.

I watched him as he shifted in his chair, appearing to stall the conversation. Then finally, he said, "My brother was here."

"He is gone, been dead for almost a year now," Hester said.

Grinning, he said, "I spend my time between Jefferson and Richmond. I never thought I'd come back to this part of Virginia, but I sort of like it here."

"You look exactly like Mr. Camm. I've never met twins who looked so much alike," Hester continued.

"People been saying that all my life," he replied and lowered his head.

I only listened to them talk. Momma was standing at the stove smiling as if she was enjoying the conversation.

My heartbeat had slowed down. I was relaxed watching Kindred as he answered Hester's questions. Most of the time, he was believable. However, there were times when he would glance away as if to prevent her from seeing through the lie he was about to tell.

Momma put biscuits on plates and we all ate them with fresh churned butter and scrambled eggs. Anything she made was tasty, and everyone appeared to be enjoying themselves, except me.

"Y'all put your clothes in the room down yonder," she said again.

"Momma, I am going to stay with Hester tonight."

"You mean to tell me you ain't staying here."

"I promised Hester I would stay with them this time."

"Suit yourself; you grown," she said.

All the time she was begging us to stay, Kindred was glancing away as if he was afraid to make eye contact. There was something about him that disturbed me. I had always been a little different. Papa said I could read things pretty good. He told me to trust my instincts. And no matter how convincing he sounded, there was something about him that was not right.

"Where are you from, Mr. Kindred?" I asked again to see if he would change his answer.

Before he could answer, Momma said, "Now, let the man eat his food. Y'all are asking questions just like Bobby do."

"Oh, I'm sorry," I said, "I was just trying to get to know him better."

"Well, all of your questions can wait 'til after we eat."

While enjoying our meal, we engaged in small talk about the church where we grew up. We discussed who was still living and who had passed away. Most importantly, I asked about Ginny, my aging aunt. Momma said, "That woman is going to outlive us all." She was tough, and mean as a snake when it was needed. No one mumbled a word about Herman Camm. It was as if he never existed. Kindred listened, but only said a few words. He was still a mystery. And it was obvious Momma did not care to know.

When we finished at Momma's, it was around 2 o'clock in the afternoon. I kissed her on the cheek goodbye and Kindred stood behind her just as Mr. Camm had done. I couldn't believe my eyes; the twins acted the same. I couldn't wait to get out of the house. Hester followed and we took off walking up the dirt road. Along the way, I complained to Hester. She listened, and came up with this crazy idea. She convinced me to stop at the Juke Joint which was hidden in the woods. Shortly after we passed the church, we made a left turn down a path. We trampled down the narrow path and through the overtaking brush that led to the Juke Joint. I had always possessed a certain curiosity about the place. The night when Momma went up there and pulled Mr. Camm out of the Joint drunk, had been as close as I had gotten to the inside of the place. Momma instructed me to sit in the buggy while she went inside. She came out with Herman Camm leaning on her like a child, so drunk he smelled of women and liquor. When he got into the buggy, the stench on him made me want to upchuck. Now, I wanted to see why folks spent their evenings drinking their sorrows away. The Joint was like the church to sinners.

We stood outside for a while, both of us gathering up courage. I inhaled deeply and stuck my breasts out like I was grown. Hester patted her long hair in place and smoothed her blouse down with her hands. It was different in the daylight than at night. The roof appeared to need work. The tin shingles on one side were loose and falling down. I wondered if the roof leaked. It was a far cry from the club where Ms. Pearl performed in Richmond. When we walked up toward the entrance, a man was standing on the outside, perhaps to greet the guests.

"How y'all ladies doing today?" he asked, grabbing the door handle and opening it for us.

"We are all right," Hester answered, and went through the door. I followed right behind her.

I was really afraid, and didn't want Momma to know about me being at the Joint. She would surely have a fit. We walked in like we had been there before and found seats at the bar beside one of Mr. Camm's old buddies, Earl. It was a lot more pleasant on the inside.

"Hi, Mr. Earl," I said, once I was seated.

"What are you doing in a place like this?" he asked.

"I suppose my curiosity brought me here, Mr. Earl."

"Y'all don't need to stay too long in a place like this. This is not for little girls."

Hester and I answered, "Yes, Sir," simultaneously, our eyes searching around trying to identify what was so attractive about this place. It was a pauper's club. Nothing cost much. The bar was made of wood, and the chairs were simply stools and barrels. I supposed it was a makeshift place where sinners could go and find refuge.

"Mr. Earl," Hester said, "you know Mr. Kindred?" Hester had heard from her father the two of them where chummy, just like he had been with Mr. Camm.

"Yea, he stops in from time to time," he said, sipping slowly on something in a liquor glass.

"He favors Mr. Camm so much, I can't tell them apart," I commented.

"Can't nobody tell that cat from his brother. They look so much alike, it is scary," he said, and took a drink.

"Does he act like him too?" Hester asked.

Mr. Earl took another sip of his drink and turned to look at me. "Now what are you two up to?"

"What do you mean?"

"You are asking a lot of questions for someone who is not up to anything."

Hester could not keep her mouth closed. She glanced over at him. "Now tell me, Mr. Earl, haven't you questioned his identity at least once?"

"Well, if you are going to be that blunt, then the answer, Chile, is yes."

"Is he Mr. Camm?"

"He says he is the brother. And I don't get into a grown man's business."

"Do you believe him?"

"Like I said, it ain't my business, but I don't have a reason not to believe him."

"Doesn't he remind you of Mr. Camm?"

"Yes he do."

I was inhaling and thinking, *I told you so.*

"Well, there were these girls we used to know; now this was before yo momma," Earl assured me. "One of them came in here one day when Kindred was up in here. He was sitting right where you are. Kindred knew her name right off the bat."

"Did she know him?"

"No, she said it was her first time knowing about a twin. She knew Camm."

"What did he say?" I asked.

"He told her Camm had described her to him."

"That sounds strange," Hester commented.

"Not really. This woman has a backside wider than the Mississippi," Earl said, grinning.

Hester and I couldn't contain ourselves; we broke out in a loud giggle.

"Now the two of you need to get out of here before the wrong person sees you and tell Mrs. Mae Lou you in here."

"Yes, Sir," I answered and slid down off the bar stool.

Then Hester had one more thing to ask. "Mr. Earl, do you think it is Mr. Camm?"

"I don't know, Chile, but I do feel most times that I am talking to a ghost."

He turned back around, took a sip of his drink and chuckled. His chuckle had me concerned.

The next day we went to visit Ginny. We arrived at her house around 10 o'clock in the morning. We had decided to stop by on the way to the train. She answered her door and was surprised to see Hester and me standing there.

"Lawd, come on in," she said and directed us into the parlor with her walking stick. "I knowed you were coming," she said. "I've been dreaming 'bout you for two days now. Usually when I dream 'bout somebody, they shows up. Make yo'self comfortable; y'all hungry?"

"No, Ma'am," I answered, and Hester said the same.

"What y'all been doing; are you planning on staying awhile?" she asked, staring at us with those mysterious green eyes.

"I'm down here on business."

"Now, what kind of bus'ness you got here in Jefferson?"

Hester answered for me, "We're trying to find out who Kindred is."

Ginny busted out in a laugh. "Join in. E'rybody wants to know about that man."

"Tell me about him, Ginny," I requested, and waited. Ginny's house had an eclectic look; nothing seemed to match. It was cozy, though, and everybody was welcomed.

"Now 'fore we get to talking about all of that, tell me this: where's my nephew?"

"I left him in Richmond."

"Well, the next time you coming down here, bring 'em to see his auntie."

"Yes, Ma'am."

"Who watching 'em for ya? Simon?"

"My neighbor downstairs."

"You talkin' 'bout the white woman I met."

"She is real good to him."

"She seems like a nice white woman. I just don't trust too many peoples."

I decided to go back to my original question. I loved Ginny, and she and I could talk all day and night long. She had been the mother I needed when I was dealing with Mr. Camm. She was the wisest woman I knew.

"Ginny, can you tell me anything about Kindred?"

"I don't know much 'bout him. He is the spitting image of that no-good Camm. He 'posed to be his twin. All I can say for sure is yo momma done took up with him. She say he is just a family member staying with her for a minute. Mae Lou is the biggest fool when it comes to men folks. Yo' papa was the best thing that ever happened to her."

"Ginny, he gives me an eerie feeling. He asked me about Robert one day and it scared me."

"You don't need to be scared of nobody. You got to stand up for yo'self. If the son-of-a-bitch say anything out of the way to you, you pick up something and bust it across his scalp. But, if he ain't bothering you, leave him alone."

"Ms. Ginny, he looks just like his brother."

"Yeah, I'm sort of concerned 'bout it myself. I ain't never seen a twin who looks just like the other one. There is always something different. One of 'em are taller or one will have a mole or something on the face. All of us make jokes and say he is Camm."

"There is something about him that disturbs me."

"You let me know if he say or do anything out of the way to you. If he didn't die the furst time, he sho' gonna die if I hear he done did you wrong."

"Ginny, will you look out for Momma for me?"

"I'll look out, but she hardheaded. You know she done fell out with Carl 'bout him. She done let that man run her own son away. Mae Lou was a fool for Herman Camm and now it seems like she a fool for Kindred Camm too."

"Do you think Momma knows anything about him?"

Ginny laughed. "She is slow, Chile, like someone done fell down and hit their head. Yo' momma knows schooling, but she don't know nothing about life. Let her be. If he do her like Camm did, then she deserve it."

CHAPTER 18

Nadine was peeking out of her window when I came down the street. I could feel her eyes on me as I walked up the stairs into the house. When I felt she was watching, I would glance in her direction and the curtain would be swaying from her quick release. She didn't want me to see her. Amazingly, Simon was in the house sitting on the davenport, relaxing, with his feet up, reading the colored newspaper, *Race and Place*. Seeing him was surprising to me, since I thought he was on the road traveling with his baseball team.

"Hi!" I said when I walked into the room.

A smile rippled across his face. "Where have you been the last two days?" he asked.

"I took a trip to Jefferson County."

"I stopped by the school. They told me you were here at the house."

"I didn't let them know where I was going. I didn't think it was their business."

He got up from the davenport and put his arms around me.

"I was worried for a minute. I thought somebody had kidnapped you," he said, smiling.

I grinned.

"Let me get your bag," he said and grabbed it out of my hand and took it into the bedroom.

I sat down on the davenport beside him. It had been a long time since Simon was home before the sun went down and was resting.

"So tell me about your trip," he said.

"I went to see Momma."

"Is she all right?"

"She is fine. She's got Kindred living with her."

"Kindred don't live in Jefferson; he is probably just visiting. Your momma don't want him. She was married to his fool of a brother, so don't get yourself riled up about that."

I didn't say anything. It was no surprise Simon wanted to believe Kindred was who he said he was. I did too, but my gut said something different. Hester and I had not come back with anything but suspicions, and it didn't prove anything. My papa had always told me to trust my instincts and I knew deep down in my soul that Kindred was none other than Herman Camm.

"Did you pick up Robert from downstairs?" I asked.

"He has been here with me for a day now. He is in the bedroom sleeping."

I went into the bedroom and Robert was still sleeping. I gazed down at him. How could someone as beautiful and innocent as Robert be connected to someone as evil as Mr. Camm? "He is still knocked out. He's been running around here all day. After I fed him, he went off to sleep." He patted the space beside him. "Come sit down. I want to talk to you."

I sat down and he put his muscular arm around my shoulders. "Tell me, why are you going from place to place trying to find out about Kindred Camm?"

I relaxed into his arms. "I'm afraid, Simon."

"You don't have any reason to be afraid. The man you see is not

Herman; it is his brother. Don't go looking for trouble." Simon didn't understand me. Kindred was more of a friend to Simon than an enemy, even though he was the mirror image of his brother. Adam had believed me the very first time. Simon tightened his arms around me and pulled me close to him. "Don't you think I can take care of you?"

"Yes," I said, knowing he couldn't take care of me if he didn't believe me.

Simon kissed me lightly on the lips and then over and over again. I succumbed to my emotions and let him roll on top of me, right on the davenport. Once he was on me, he unbuttoned my dress and pulled down my bloomers. We both were panting like dogs. He got on me and I didn't think to get my sponge. He entered my moistness and I began to groan. Just as we were about to explode, I begged Simon to withdraw because I could not hold my urine. I really couldn't risk getting pregnant. And I knew it was something Simon desired.

Just when we were tired and beads of sweat dripped off our brows, someone knocked on the door. Simon and I quickly put on our clothing. I went into the bathroom and Simon went to answer the door. When I returned from the bathroom and went into the kitchen, I saw Nadine's little girl standing in the kitchen with a cup in one hand. She appeared to be handing Simon a note with the other.

"What is it you need?" I said.

"My momma sent me over here to get a cup of sugar."

I took the cup out of her hand, opened the sugar canister and dipped out a cup of sugar. I handed the cup back to her. She said, "Thank you," and left.

Simon went out the door behind her, stood on the porch and

watched her cross the street. After she went in her house, he came into the kitchen.

"Did I see her give you something?"

He raised his voice annoyed. "Give me something? You must be seeing things."

"Simon, I saw her hand you something."

"She didn't hand me anything," he claimed, without blinking.

I knew what I had seen. I didn't understand why Simon was lying to me again.

I turned around and walked back into the sitting area. I sat down on the davenport and waited for him to come in. He never came. After a couple of minutes, I walked back into the kitchen. He was stuffing a piece of balled-up paper into his pocket.

My lips were sealed. I never let on that I had seen the paper; I knew he would only deny it. He gazed me in the face and not one frown was on his face. He had what the gamblers called a poker face. I could not tell what the note contained by his expression. Again, Nadine had disrespected me.

"I've got to run out for a few minutes," he said, glancing at the wall clock. "I hope you don't mind."

I looked at him, shook my head, and walked back into the bedroom to check on Robert. He was still sleep. Simon went into the bathroom, washed up and headed out the door.

I watched from the window as he got into his car, which was parked outside, turned it around and headed up the street in the direction of the club. I sat in the window seat and watched from a gap in the curtains as the sun went down. I was just about to leave and go to bed when I noticed Nadine come out her front door and walk in the direction of the club.

Beads of sweat popped up on the brow of my nose—something that happened whenever I was angry. I wanted to see what was going on, but I had Robert. I sat down on the davenport and everything came to mind. The more I thought about it, the angrier I became. After thinking about it for ten minutes, I woke Robert up. I took him downstairs and left him with the Halls. As usual, they were happy to watch him. Mrs. Hall gazed me in the eyes. "Something is bothering you, Child."

"I'm all right, Mrs. Hall."

"Well, don't let whatever it is get the best of you."

"I won't," I promised her, and left.

It was chilly at night in Richmond. With spring approaching, daytime temperatures had been mild, but at night, the frost would settle on the ground. It was fine because I was sweating. I briskly walked toward the club without knowing what I might find. All I knew was that something was going on and I was going to find out what it was.

When I made it to the club, I saw Simon's car parked in front. I inhaled to garner up the nerve necessary to confront whatever was going on. The night was young, and there were a few patrons going inside. Ms. Pearl was not performing.

I walked inside the club and took a seat at a small table in the corner. I wanted to be incognito, so I attempted to blend in. The table was away from the lights, and I sat there waiting. I glanced around at the patrons. There were a few women dressed up with face powder on and vibrant pink and red lipstick. A couple of men dressed in suits were standing around the bar. The bartender, as usual, was standing in front of them talking. I did not see Simon anywhere, and Nadine wasn't in sight, either. For a minute, I was at ease. But it didn't last long.

"Ma'am, you want something to drink?" the bartender asked and scared me, since I never saw him walk up. He had two roles—bartender and waiter.

"I'll take a glass of water," I said, even though I could have used a drink, like the other sinners who had drowned their problems with liquor. I was not a drinker, though.

It wasn't long before the bartender came back with my water. I sat there listening to the music playing. The longer I sat, the more relaxed I became. I sipped on the ice water and took interest in everything going on around me. The men in suits walked over to the table where the three women were seated and started to chat. The longer they sat there, the louder their voices became. It wasn't long before sounds were reverberating from all over the place. The room was coming alive.

I sat there for over an hour before I decided to leave. Simon's car was there, but he was nowhere to be found. As I got up to leave, Simon walked from the back of the room with Nadine following close behind him. I watched as he kissed her on the cheek and escorted her to the door, but before they got there, I had gotten up. My blood was boiling. I walked over to them with my water in my hand and tossed the entire glass of water on the both of them. Nadine started to buck up at me, but I didn't scare. She lowered her eyes and ran out the door instead. Water was dripping from her face.

"It is not what you think!" Simon yelled. "I'm soaked and wet, Girl," he said, brushing water off his shirt with his hands.

I didn't say anything. I stood there with a scowl on my face, my chest heaving.

He pulled out his handkerchief and wiped the water off his face. "Can we talk, Carrie?"

"Yes, when you are ready to tell the truth," I answered, and threw my head up. All of a sudden, I had become fearless, ready for him.

He put his hand on my arm. I shook it off, set the empty glass on the table, and walked out.

I didn't go straight home. I went to Nadine's. I knocked on the door and waited for someone to answer. The little girl opened the door.

"Is your momma here?"

"My momma is not home," she said.

"Well, I'll just come in and wait for her." I pushed open the door and stepped inside. The girl's eyes popped wide open.

"No, she ain't here. You got to go home," the little girl said, attempting to coax me back out of the door.

"Go get your momma. I am not leaving."

Ten seconds later, Nadine walked into her sitting room. Her hands were trembling with fear. "Carrie, you need to leave. I don't want you in my house," Nadine said and then crossed her arms over her chest.

"I'm not going nowhere. You are going to tell me what is going on with you and my husband."

"I told you we are just friends!" she argued, raising her voice to a level of intimidation.

"If all that you say is true, then why won't you talk to me?"

"Carrie, you need to leave right now."

I walked toward her and she backed up. Her children stood around listening.

"Y'all, go into your bedroom," she told them.

Her son left and went back down the hallway. Her daughter did not move.

"Sammie, go on into your room, I said!" she yelled, but the daughter stubbornly stood there.

"Nadine, you need to tell me why you were with my husband tonight."

She unfolded her arms and swung them by her side. She was nervous and it was obvious on her face, which had frown lines across her forehead.

"I don't want to talk about it. You need to ask Simon your questions."

I was getting tired of reasoning with her. I moved closer to her. I was about to push her down on the davenport when her little girl got in between us. "You can't come into our house. You leave!" she yelled.

"I will go when your mother tells me the truth."

"Like I told you, I've known Simon a long time. I knew him when I was thirteen years old, before I had any children, and my oldest is nine now."

"You are no-good trash, Nadine. You have no respect for me as his wife and I am sick of you!" I yelled.

"Get out! You can't talk to me like that; this is my damn house."

I turned to walk away, but could not leave. My fists were balled up waiting for her to make a move toward me, but all she did was stand in the corner swinging her arms nervously. She was upset, and I was determined to make her tell me the truth.

"I'm not going anywhere until you tell me why you were with my husband tonight."

She yelled, "I had to borrow some money from him. Is that all right?"

"No, you have a man, so why don't ask him for it?"

"I needed it right away."

The little girl was standing watching as teardrops trickled down her cheeks.

"Oh, Ma, just tell her!" the little girl sang out.

"Go to your room," Nadine demanded, but the child wouldn't move.

"What is it she wants to tell me?" I asked.

"Nothing; just leave," Nadine said.

"Little girl, tell me what is going on here."

Nadine interjected, "You need to go. If you won't leave, then I will. Sammie, go tell your brother to come on."

"I'm not," the child replied.

When Nadine tried to grab her hand, she pulled back and yelled, "Simon is my daddy!"

I didn't expect to hear what she'd said. I stood there gazing at Nadine, waiting for a reaction.

"Now are you happy? He is my children's father."

I went numb. All of a sudden, I was speechless. I didn't have a comeback.

I walked out the door, and went across the street. I didn't look back. I walked past the front door of the Halls' apartment and kept going straight up the stairs. I didn't know what to think, but I had witnessed a certain relief in the little girl's eyes once she'd blurted out the truth. I left Nadine in the sitting room with her arms around Simon's little girl, who was crying like a baby. I was mad as hell.

CHAPTER 19

I felt defeated when I left Nadine's house. I went home, sat on the davenport and peered out the window waiting for Simon's car to come down the street. I fell asleep anxious to talk to him about the things I'd found out. He owed me some answers. I was his wife. How on earth did he think we could live across the street from them and I wouldn't find out about his other family? After he didn't show up, I found myself wiping teardrops from my eyes.

When he did finally show up the next day, he acted as if I had done something to him. He walked past me in the kitchen and did not say a word. I shook my head. How dare he? Then he went into the bathroom, slammed the door and took a bath, dressed, and left the house without parting his lips. Once he was gone, I emptied every drawer in the chiffonier, stuffed all the clothes he owned into the duffle bag he traveled with, and put it at the door. I was young and naïve, but I was not his fool.

I told Mrs. Hall about what I had experienced. She said, "You worry about yourself; don't worry about Simon. He can take care of himself."

She didn't seem surprised at all about what I told her Nadine had said. Mr. Hall listened in his high-back wooden rocking chair as I told my story. He didn't say anything, yet when I said children, he grunted.

"Mr. Hall, did you know they were Simon's children?"

He hesitated and then answered, "I wouldn't pay too much attention to what folks say. I would talk to Simon. Some things are better dealt with in private."

He was right. I felt the same way.

Mrs. Hall cut her eyes his way. "We are her family. She don't have nobody else to turn to. Now you and me need to help her deal with all of this."

"The best thing we can do is care for Robert. He is the innocent one in all of this," Mr. Hall said.

I peered at him. "I didn't do anything, Mr. Hall."

"Oh, Child, I didn't mean it in a bad way. It's just that Robert didn't ask for it, but he is in the middle of a family crisis."

"I don't understand," I said.

"Your son needs a father. There are things a woman cannot do for a boy child. After all of this, things are bound to be different."

I felt Mr. Hall was taking up for Simon in a way. He still believed Simon and I would be together.

"We will cross that bridge if we have to," Mrs. Hall commented.

"What should I do, Mrs. Hall?" I inquired, rubbing my forehead because I had a dull headache.

"You should continue with your schooling."

"What about Simon?" I asked her, but she just shook her head.

"You need to do something to get your mind off of things. Stop by and get Hester and y'all go and listen to good jazz sounds tonight," Mrs. Hall said. "I can remember when we were young and making decisions about our relationship, I would always go to a little tea room around the corner and listen to the band play. Music has its way with the blues."

I smiled. "Robert is always here. He barely knows me."

"He knows you. He is just more familiar with us," Mr. Hall said.

Mrs. Hall got up from the davenport and walked over to her husband. She rubbed his shoulders. "We love having a child in the house."

Mr. Hall looked back at her and smiled. I knew Robert was in good hands, and now I could tell by their reactions how much they loved him.

When I got up to leave, Mrs. Hall pulled me close against her bosom and hugged me as if I was her child. It was the best feeling to me, so I laid my head in her arms and the tears slid uncontrollably down my cheeks.

"Go on upstairs and get dressed. Go out and have a good time. Remember this event will be history soon."

I shook my head. I kissed Robert goodbye as he was playing on the floor. I saw Nadine as I was walking back up the stairs to my apartment. I threw my head up in the air, and inhaled to keep calm. I went into my house and peeped out the window. She was standing on her porch gazing over at my house. After a minute, she turned and went into the house.

I had listened to the Halls, yet I still found myself angry and hurt. When I glanced over at Nadine's house, I was tempted to go over there again, get in her face and make her feel like the slut she was, but I couldn't. All I could think about were the times she had come to my house begging for sugar or butter just because she wanted to be in the company of my husband. Now she claimed her children are Simon's. I didn't see the resemblance, but I never paid any attention to them.

CHAPTER 20

Hester was glad to go along with me to the club. She was starting to enjoy the city life and the activity at the club. She had said a mouthful. "If I see Simon, I am going to say a few words to him myself. He ought to be ashamed of himself; no wonder he didn't come home. Nadine ain't nothing but a floozy. I'll bet those kids don't belong to Simon. She probably doesn't know who the daddy is."

"I'm so tired thinking about it," I said, standing in the line to enter the club.

"Did you see his car when we walked up?"

I looked around. "I don't know where he is. His vehicle is not around here. You know I believe he cares more about that Model T than me."

"Maybe he really is gone to play ball this time."

"I can't believe a word he says these days," I said, peering around, hoping Simon would walk up at any time.

"I'll bet your brothers would be shocked to learn about him. I know John would be in his face."

"I don't want them to know."

"I don't understand why you are protecting him. He didn't think enough of you to tell you the truth. I just can't believe the children story."

"I believe her. Her little girl told me."

Hester sighed. "It is a shame when a child has more sense than an adult."

"The little girl was determined to tell me. She would not leave the room."

"Carrie, we've been friends for a long time. I am so sorry for the things you've had to go through. I just hope now you can move forward without all the unnecessary mess."

"Keep your voice down," I whispered. "I don't want any of these people in my business. You know how fast gossip travels."

"They don't know you," she whispered back in my ear.

"I know. I don't want them to staring at me. I must be the biggest fool in Jackson Heights."

"I doubt it. Nadine is the biggest fool. She is living across the street from her children's daddy and secretly wanting to take your place. Now, that is crazy. I've heard it all."

I glanced over at her. "What am I going to do?"

"We're going in here tonight and listen to the sounds and try to be happy. We can pray about the rest of it later. If Simon comes in here tonight, just ignore him. I have something I want to say to him."

"Hester, I'm scared."

"Oh, this will pass soon enough."

When the door to the club opened, everybody seemed to come alive. I wish there was another club around where people hung out. I wasn't sure if I could handle seeing Nadine or Simon. Mrs. Hall said music could heal me, so I went into the club expecting to feel good.

It was the first time I'd been to the club and didn't see Mrs. Maggie Walker and her companion sitting front and center. She had reserved seating. Someone else was sitting at her table. The seats filled up fast. And, to my surprise, Adam Murphy was there.

He spotted me from across the floor and came over to the table in the middle of the floor where Hester and I were seated.

"Hi, Carrie; it's nice seeing you here." He reached over to shake Hester's hand. "And, Hester, it is nice to see you again too." His politeness was one of his most admirable traits. He knew what it meant to care.

"Hi," I said.

He pulled out a chair. "I will only be here a minute," he explained, looking at Hester as if she was the one to get approval from.

"Stay for a while," Hester said.

"No, I'm here with a friend from school. We needed a break."

"I thought you were still in Petersburg," I said.

"I came home today, and will be going back on the first train Monday morning."

"Me too."

"It's not so bad down in Petersburg. The school is good for me and I love the slower pace."

People were coming in the door like they did the night Bessie Smith was in town. The white man Ms. Pearl was always with was seated at the bar. He appeared to be watching everybody entering the club, like he was sizing them up. He glanced up whenever someone walked through the door. And I noticed how he peered directly in their faces. He'd then take a sip from his glass and glance around the room. Something was up. Maybe Ms. Bessie was back in town.

I was also sizing up the crowd. My eyes were fixated on the door, watching to see if any famous people were entering the club. The crowd seemed jovial and active. I was determined to enjoy myself, even though I couldn't get Nadine and Simon off my mind. Now I finally had Adam's full attention, but it was not him I was concerned about.

"You seem to be someplace else, Carrie," Adam said, peering across the table at me with his dark eyes.

"It's the crowd. I guess I'm a little overwhelmed," I lied.

He got up. "Well, it's nice seeing you, Carrie," he said, and walked away.

"I don't understand how you can be so hung up on Simon when you have a friend like Adam," Hester said, shaking her head.

"I'm not hung up on him; he is my husband. Adam is a wonderful man, but I want to be sure before I give in to him."

"Don't take too long. The women are noticing him as we speak."

I glanced across the room at Adam, and two beautiful ladies were standing in front of the table where he was seated talking, smiling and flirting.

"They are smiling like Cheshire cats. Things couldn't be that good," I commented.

"You sound like you're jealous," Hester said, grinning.

"I'm not jealous. I just think he needs a special type of friend."

"One like you..."

"Hester, I'm trying to deal with Simon. We are supposed to be enjoying the music."

"I'm having a good time watching the sights. Have you noticed how the white man at the bar is looking at everybody coming through the door?" Hester asked.

"There is something strange going on. I just hope nobody will get hurt," I said, looking around making sure we were safe.

"What do you mean?"

"He is the same man who pulled the gun on Willie and shot him. I really believe he is some sort of gangster. He is always around Ms. Pearl and the rumor is, he owns this club, right in the heart of a colored neighborhood."

"He may be Ms. Pearl's manager. Big-time singers always have someone to look over their business, to make sure they are treated right," Hester said.

"Maybe he is that to her. I came to see Simon one day and he was in the back room with Ms. Pearl and that man," I whispered. "They had money on the table."

"Did you ask Simon who the white man is?" Hester asked.

"No, but I could tell he was the man in charge. It was the way he acted; I knew he was running things."

"It's a lot of people in here," Hester said, looking around at all the people in the building. Most of the men seemed to hang around the bar, and the women were all seated. The men were dressed in suits and hats and the women had on low-waist chiffon dresses of all colors, silk stockings and lots of face powder and rouge on their cheeks. The table lanterns reflected the shadows on the walls. People appeared to be everywhere. The bartender was busy. He was an occasional waiter and server as well. He did it all. The phonograph was playing music, although most people were talking. A few sat at their tables bouncing their heads back and forth. It was a lively place.

"I'm enjoying myself," Hester leaned over and said.

"Me too, I guess," I answered.

I peered over to the other side of the room at Adam and he was staring straight at me. I waved at him. He nodded his head, and to my surprise, threw me a kiss. I quickly turned my head to make sure no one was looking at us. Everybody was having their own private conversations. No one seemed to notice me.

"Did he just throw you a kiss?" Hester asked, smiling from ear to ear.

"I'm not paying him any attention," I replied.

"You are, and I'll bet you have forgotten about Simon already."

I smiled and playfully rolled my eyes at her comments. We glanced at one another and broke out laughing. There was a lot going on; everyone had some action of their own. The ladies at the table in front of us were joined by two handsome men. Now they were giggling and one of the men had his arm around the shoulder of the lady in the blue dress. The men at the bar had drinks in their hands. A couple of them had cigars in between their fingers. And, in the back of the room was a couple embracing and kissing as if they were at home in private. We were not the only people staring at them. After a while, the white man walked over to them and they immediately let go of each other and found a seat.

"When do you think Ms. Pearl is going to come out?"

"Once everybody is settled, she'll come in and all attention will turn to her. That's what always happens," I said, tapping my fingers on the table.

Hester shook her head. "I think the two of us are stealing the attention. Take a look at the two fellows in the corner; they have been watching us ever since they came in the door. And one of them is sort of cute."

I glanced over at the two men. "I hope they don't come over here."

"Why can't you loosen up and have a little fun? Simon is nowhere to be found."

"I don't want to think about him. I just want to let the music heal me," I said.

Hester rolled her eyes.

Before I could say another word, Ms. Pearl came from the back room and strolled slowly to the stage. Along the way, she stopped several times to greet some of the patrons. She was dressed in a beautiful lavender dress, which fit her like a glove. She seemed to roll her hips with each stride she took. Men and women alike admired her. The women whispered about her fashionable dress and the men studied her body as if it were on display solely for them.

Her band came out and made it to the stage before Ms. Pearl was halfway through the crowd. It was so well put together. They grabbed their instruments and serenaded her to the stage. Hester sat with her mouth wide open in total amazement. When Ms. Pearl strolled past my table, she leaned over. "It is nice to see you girls again." Both of us smiled, and I waved.

"She spoke to us!" Hester said, still grinning.

"I know," I said, waiting for the show to start.

Just as the music changed for Ms. Pearl, I noticed Kindred across the room. He was staring at Ms. Pearl.

"Kindred's here," I whispered to Hester.

"I saw him when he followed Ms. Pearl out from the back of the club."

Surprisingly, I had not noticed him at all. I suppose my eyes were focused on Ms. Pearl and how she wooed the crowd even before she took the microphone.

When Ms. Pearl started to sing, the entire crowd broke out in thunderous applause for her. Some of the patrons stood up. I was clapping so hard, the insides of my hands were pink. Hester was having a great time, and was swaying back and forth.

Kindred Camm was dressed just like his brother. His suit fit him like a glove, as if it was especially made for him. He had on a fedora, like the one the white man had on. He had a drink in his hand and was standing near the bar, leaning on the wall, admiring Ms. Pearl's performance. Her white friend was also admiring her. He had turned around at the bar and was sitting with his eyes focused on Ms. Pearl.

"Here, I brought you something to drink." Adam had two Coca-Colas in his hand. He put one in front of me and the other in front of Hester. He then pulled out a chair and took a seat.

"Do you girls mind if I sit here for a second?"

There was something special about Adam. He had the ability to make me feel special, even if it was with a soda pop.

"Thank you for the drink, Adam," Hester said before taking a swallow.

"How did you know I was thirsty?" I said.

"I know a lot about you. I know the things you tell and the things you don't say," he whispered in my ear.

"What are you talking about?"

"Something is on your mind tonight. I can tell."

"I'm okay," I said.

"You can't fool me. If you need anybody to talk to, I'm here for you."

Adam was more in tune with my emotions than my husband. It was the thing I liked about him. I loved the way he gazed at me and how he could sense my troubles. I wondered if he was what people called a soulmate.

I shook my head yes to Adam. He smiled. We both refocused on Ms. Pearl, who was swaying from side to side. She was bellowing out sounds we wanted to hear. She had her head back and eyes closed, but when she opened them, she stared straight at Kindred. He did not move, just grinned and stared back at her. It was like they were connected in some way. The lady at the table in front of us said out loud, "She's got a thing for him."

The white fellow raised out of his seat. He moved through the crowd until he was right beside Kindred.

"Did you see that?" Hester asked.

"It looks like they are arguing."

Kindred and the man were standing toe to toe. The white man pushed Kindred.

"Come on, Carrie; it is time to get you out of here," Adam said, as he pulled me through the crowd toward the door. Hester was right behind me holding my other hand. We didn't want to get separated. Right before we made it to the door, a scuffle caused people to panic and everyone started to charge forward toward the door. Adam pulled me and I pulled Hester. We made it to the door just as a shot rang out in the club. I turned to look and all I could see was the white man standing with a gun.

"Don't look back," Adam warned us.

We kept walking until we were at least 200 feet from the club. Another shot was fired. When we turned to look back, there was a man lying on the ground. A lady was bending over him crying out loud, "He was just looking at her!"

Adam and I walked Hester home first, and then he walked me home. I cried the entire way.

"You gonna be all right?" Adam asked me.

"I hope so."

Adam stood on my porch and then kissed me on the lips.

"Remember, I'm here for you," he said, before walking away. "See you at school."

It made me sad to see him leave. I went inside my apartment, got undressed and crawled in the bed. Simon was not home, as usual. It was yet another night I was alone. I couldn't believe I had witnessed another shooting at the same club. For some reason, I felt it was about Ms. Pearl. Momma had warned me she was trouble.

Teardrops beat against my pillow. I cried for the injured and mostly for me. I prayed Adam would make it home safely.

CHAPTER 21

School was my refuge. I stayed at school two weeks straight without even considering coming home. When I finally decided it was time to go home, I caught the midday train. I was glad to see the tall, handsome, dark man on the train. It was as if he was there to give me a message. Immediately, I thought about how much he looked like my papa, and just maybe papa was saying, "I am watching over you." The man was kind and when he smiled, it was the same way my papa had smiled before he died.

For those two weeks, while I had been in Petersburg, I had avoided Adam. I had too much on my mind. I didn't want to confuse my feeling for him with the ones I still had for Simon. I couldn't do such a thing to him. He deserved much more. I had to clear my head of all the garbage, including the night at the club, and make a decision as to where I was going in my life.

Simon was home when I opened the door. He was sitting in the kitchen sipping on a cup of coffee, gazing out of the window as if he was waiting for someone. He saw me and jumped up. "I was wondering if you were going to come home. You hungry?" he asked.

"No," I replied. I had expected him to be gone.

"I know you don't want to talk to me," he said, reaching for my suitcase.

I smacked my lips, and sighed. "Simon, you left, not me."

"You put my clothes at the door."

I walked out of the kitchen.

"Are you coming back?!" he yelled.

"Maybe," I said and went into the bathroom. When I came out, he was sitting on the davenport with the coffee in his hand.

I sat in the high-back chair across from him.

He appeared nervous, scratched his head and said, "I've messed up, haven't I?"

I could feel the tension rising inside me. "Simon, you have a family living right across the street. I guess I'm supposed to be all right with that?"

"Naw, it wasn't 'posed to be like it look," he said, running his fingers through his hair.

"Well, what do I need to know?" I said and waited.

"The children came when I was just a little boy myself."

I bit my bottom lip, and tried to think about what he'd just said. Papa used to say, it is best to keep quiet and listen. Now I was trying to force myself to listen to a story I didn't want to hear.

"Are you going to talk?" he asked me, so humble I had to look away from him. I had to gather myself; my emotions were surfacing. Teardrops were creeping out the corners of my eyes, even though I did all I could to keep them from dripping down my cheeks. I wiped the corners of my eyes with my finger.

I coughed, and cleared my throat. "Simon, I don't know what to say."

"I want you to know, I don't care about Nadine," he blurted out.

"Nadine has been in our lives ever since I've been in Richmond. She uses whatever means she can to get a glimpse of you. She's taken my milk, butter and sugar, just to get into your house. She didn't need any of it, because you've been taking care of her. I've even caught her in my apartment with you. Tell the truth, Simon, the truth…"

He shook his head. "It isn't what you think. I don't want Nadine."

"She is the mother of your children. She's in your life no matter what now."

He stood up. I could see the frustration on his face. His face was tight and frown lines were around his lips and across his forehead. "I just want you to hear me, Carrie," he said, swinging his arms like he needed to get my attention.

"Are you serious?" I asked, "This is crazy. Nadine and your two children live directly across the street from your wife and her son. Is that how things should be?"

He sat back down. "Now listen, I only agreed for them to be across the street because I wanted to make sure the children were all right. Nadine can sometimes forget to care for them."

"She seems to do all right to me."

He had every excuse imaginable concerning the matter. Looking after the children made plenty of sense to me, but who in their right mind did things that way. I know he thought I was country, naïve and young, but all things considered, I was not a fool. He must have thought I was too stupid to find out the truth. Papa always preached that the truth would eventually come out. I just didn't figure it was living across the street.

"Were you going to say anything?"

"I guess at some point," he said, with his head lowered.

"Simon, you and Nadine have been out of town together."

"Now, folks are lying on me. I ain't been nowhere with Nadine."

I wanted to put my hands over my ears. I had heard from more than one person he'd been riding around Petersburg with a woman in the car. He had denied ever being in Petersburg, had proclaimed he was playing ball. Now he was telling me people were lying on him. Simon was a convincing man. I had believed him for a long time, but now I could tell he was lying.

"More than one person has seen you with her. I even saw you myself."

His eyes appeared to recede into his head, and all of a sudden they were slits. He was out of balance and I could see his uneasiness. He adjusted himself in the chair. "When did you see me?"

"I saw you drop her off the other day. You had her and the children in the car."

"I gave them a ride from downtown."

"I thought I knew you, Simon. I thought you were honest and just a plain country boy with big dreams. I really don't know you anymore. You are in the club when you are supposed to be traveling with the Colored League, chasing after Mr. Pete Hill. Instead, you are with family, the one I didn't know about. I am as confused as you are, Simon. I thought you loved me."

He stood back up and began pacing the floor.

"Why can't you understand me?" I asked.

"I have never said anything about Robert to you."

All of a sudden my tone changed, and I started to shake. "When you married me, you knew the entire story. I have never lied to you about him. You never said anything about a family in Richmond. Does your sister, Mary, know about your other life?"

He paced the floor. "No, she don't know about it. Nadine didn't tell me until my daughter was born that she was mine."

"So what, you've made a mistake. What about your son?" I could feel the steam rising up in me.

He sat down. "We got back together before I met you, and she got pregnant again. I wasn't trying to have more children with Nadine."

"Nadine has been disrespecting me since day one. If I had known about the children, I think it wouldn't have hurt as bad."

"Look now, Nadine told me she saw you with Adam just the other night."

"Where were you, Simon...at her house peeping out the window?" I got up. "He walked me home, since my husband was nowhere to be found."

He didn't comment.

"I'm tired of talking about it. I'm going to bed," I said.

I left him sitting there. I went into the bedroom and locked the door. It was a sad night for me. I couldn't blame the children; they didn't ask to be in the middle of confusion. I blamed Simon for being able to lie as easily as the blink of an eye.

CHAPTER 22

The colored newspaper confirmed Kindred Camm was dead. I couldn't believe he had died before I found out the true identity of the Camm twin. Everybody in town and all over Jefferson County was gossiping, so Hester said. I had escaped most of the chatter after the crime by those two weeks I had remained in Petersburg. Everyone was curious about Kindred. The owner of the corner store said, "Did you hear about that boy that got killed down at the club?"

Another man in the store replied, "Yeah, I heard. They say the boy was dirty." Nobody understood or knew why he was murdered. He was the mystery man. No one really knew anything about him, and now everyone wanted to know about the mysterious twin. I especially wanted to know.

The Halls, Robert and I climbed into Simon's car. We were close, like sardines in a can. Curiosity had everybody wanting to see if Kindred Camm was really a twin. Folks were saying the white man called him a phony Negro, but with all the noise in the club, how could anyone really know. The night they'd had words, he'd called him Herman, folks said. Several people claimed to have overheard it, and now everyone desired to know the truth. People from Jackson Heights were traveling to Jefferson in droves to see the funeral of a man nobody really knew.

182 RUTH P. WATSON

We arrived in Jefferson County exactly an hour before the funeral. Momma was in her room getting dressed when we got there. An attractive and distinctive, caramel-colored, middle-aged lady stood in Momma's parlor. She was a stranger to us. When she opened the door to welcome us, everyone appeared to be surprised. Momma never allowed strangers to answer her door.

"Mae Lou is in the other room getting dressed. Y'all come on in," she said in a sophisticated Southern drawl.

I reached my hand out to her. She shook my hand and smiled. We all greeted her and took a seat. When we had taken a seat, she told us who she was.

"I'm Elizabeth Camm. I am Kindred's wife."

Mrs. Hall hastily said, "So sorry for your loss."

"Thank you," she replied.

Our eyes moved from one to another. "Is something wrong?" she asked.

"No, we just didn't know Kindred was married."

"Yeah, we've been together for over twenty years. We met in secondary school. We didn't have any children, though."

Nobody commented. Everybody just sat there and waited for Momma to finish getting dressed. It was a warm day for a home-going. The aroma of ham and biscuits tantalized our senses.

"I'm hungry," Simon commented and went into the kitchen.

It wasn't long before Momma came into the room all dressed up in her black funeral dress and the hat the church members admired, which she'd sewn herself. Her eyes were bloodshot, as if she'd been drinking liquor. Surely she had been crying, which was more than she'd done for my papa. She looked as fine as Mrs. Elizabeth did who was as sharp a dresser as Ms. Maggie Walker. I couldn't imagine the conversation they might have had the night before about the Camm men.

"Hi, everybody. Before we leave for the church, anybody want something to eat?"

"Simon was looking for something," I said.

"Anybody else?"

She turned around and went back into the kitchen. It was not long before Simon came back in the parlor with a ham biscuit wrapped in paper. He said he'd eat it on the drive to the church, which was right up the road.

We couldn't all fit in the car, so Momma and Mrs. Hall road in the buggy. Mrs. Hall was fascinated with the country, and riding to the church in the buggy was a treat.

"The undertaker came and picked up Kindred and took him to the church last night," Momma said.

When my papa had passed on, his body had sat in the parlor for over a week. It wasn't until he'd started to smell that we'd had the service. The deacons came for his body the day of the funeral. Kindred probably had never been inside a church.

The rest of us, including Mrs. Camm, piled into the car and headed toward the church. It was a short ride. And I could remember walking there many times.

The church was full of people. Ginny was the first person I saw. She stood on the church steps and waited for me. I couldn't wait to give her a hug and let Robert get to know his aunt. Ginny knew everybody except Mrs. Elizabeth.

"Hi, I'm Carrie's aunt," Ginny said and examined Mrs. Elizabeth from top to bottom. Her piercing green eyes were intimidating to most. Mrs. Elizabeth partially shook Ginny's hand as if she had a disease and walked up the steps and into the church.

"I need to come in with the family. I need to take a look at my husband and say goodbye. I haven't seen him in over two years," she said with tears in her eyes.

We all took a seat close to the front of the church. Ms. Pearl was sitting up front alongside the bartender from the club. Everybody came to the funeral except for my brothers, who hated both Camms. The church was packed.

Mrs. Elizabeth stood at the casket for a long time. She was studying the body like a doctor would. She bent down to take a look at his chin. She appeared to be examining his hairline. She had to slide to the side twice to allow two other people to get a view of the body. As soon as the preacher stood up in the pulpit, she screamed, "Lawd have mercy!" Simon and several other men ran toward her.

"Lawd, Lawd, Lawd!" Mrs. Elizabeth sang out.

"Ma'am, what is wrong?" one of the men asked. Simon was holding her up, afraid she was going to tumble over into the coffin.

"This is not my Kindred!" she cried out.

Chatter broke out in the church. Ms. Pearl got up and walked up to the coffin. She stood staring down at the corpse.

"What is going on?" Pearl asked.

"This is not my husband." The preacher grabbed one of her arms and Simon held onto the other.

You could hear echoes all over the church. "Who is it then?"

Ms. Pearl mumbled, "It looks like Kindred to me." Some of the men in the church smiled. Their wives cut an evil eye toward them and the smile disappeared.

She yelled, "This is Herman! Where is my Kindred?" Folks got up from their seats and moved closer to get a good look. The churchgoers were talking so loudly, it sounded like a party.

The preacher cleared his throat. "Now y'all calm down; this is the Lawd's house!"

The chatter started to diminish. The sounds were fading until Mrs. Elizabeth fainted, and fell to the floor. Folks came running;

some tried to revive her and others stood looking in the casket to see if they recognized the corpse. Momma had her head hung low. Ginny nudged me in the side. "Yo momma doesn't look surprised."

The preacher clapped and finally got the folks' attention. Simon and Mr. Earl took Mrs. Elizabeth out after someone put some ammonia under her nose to sniff, and her eyes swung open.

"We gonna give this man a proper burial," the preacher said.

He began to preach. The entire church added an "amen" and "aha," and then one of the sisters in the church choir sang a hymn. It was a quick service. Momma sat still, like she was hypnotized, staring at the casket. Around us, folks were whispering. A woman glanced over at Momma and shook her head. Momma shielded her face and looked in the opposite direction.

On the way home from the cemetery, no one said a word. Mrs. Elizabeth stared out the window at the cows in the field, tears streaming down her cheeks.

Aunt Bessie had prepared a mini feast when we made it back to the house. She had fried chicken, potatoes, green beans, fried corn and a cake for dessert. Simon glanced over at me with a strange smirk on his face. Mrs. Hall didn't say one word, and Mrs. Elizabeth just sat in the chair wiping tears.

Ginny had ridden back with Momma. After the table was blessed and we started to prepare the plates, she just said it. "Mae Lou, did you know that man was Herman?"

"I don't think this is a good time to talk about it," Momma said.

"When is a good time?" Mrs. Elizabeth fired back, wiping her eyes.

Ginny said, "I think you knew it was Herman. So, the one who was killed over a year ago was Kindred. How in hell did this happen?"

Mrs. Elizabeth stood up. "I'll tell you."

"Gw'on and tell us," Ginny coaxed.

"My Kindred was always taking up for his low-down, dirty

brother, Herman. Herman would always get hisself mixed up in things and then come running to my Kindred to help him fight his battles. You knew, Mae Lou; you knew."

"I didn't make Kindred do nothing."

"Mae Lou, I never thought you'd love a man so much, you'd forsake the whole entire fam'ly," Ginny commented.

Momma said, "I ain't have nothing to do with all of this.'"

"Y'all leave her alone. She is probably going through something too," Aunt Bessie said, defending her sister.

"My Kindred died because people mistake him for Herman. They looked too much alike."

"Ms. Elizabeth, how could you tell the difference?" I asked.

"Herman didn't have a mole on his right hand. Kindred had a big ole mole there. That man didn't have one and his hairline was a little thinner than my Kindred. Now which one of y'all killed my husband?"

"Now, Ma'am, we didn't kill your husband," Simon said. "He got his own self killed. Folks thought he was Herman."

"I've got to get out of here. I don't trust none of y'all," she said, walking toward the bedroom.

Ginny glanced over at Momma. "See, Mae Lou, what you done? You got the entire family messed up. Why couldn't you just leave that bastard alone?"

Momma stood up. "Ginny, you need to finish that plate you are eating and get out of my house. You have always been meddling in my business. Find something to do. Make a quilt or something, but leave me the hell alone."

Ginny pointed her cane. "I will go up beside yo' head, Woman. Simon, I need you to take me home."

"We all might as well go on back home," Mr. Hall commented.

Mrs. Elizabeth came out of the room with her bags. "You mind if I squeeze in the car? I can catch the train back to D.C. I want to stop and see Pearl Brown."

I couldn't believe what had happened. I knew it was Herman from the beginning, yet no one believed me. We all got ready to leave. Momma was sitting in the kitchen. Aunt Bessie was with her. I whispered in Aunt Bessie's ear. "Please take care of her. She is hurting."

"I will," she said.

I handed Robert to Momma, who had been quiet the entire time. She kissed him on the cheek and for the first time, I saw her shed tears.

"I'll see you soon," I said.

"Don't stay away too long. Carrie, I'm sorry," she said.

I shook my head yes, and held my hands out for Robert. We walked out of the kitchen and Momma didn't even move. I sat on Mrs. Hall's lap until we dropped Ginny off. Ginny had been holding Robert. Afterward, I got in the front seat of the vehicle. I had a headache. Again, Momma had let me down.

CHAPTER 23

Mrs. Elizabeth asked to be dropped off at the club. Simon and I insisted upon waiting for her in the car. She was not in there five minutes before she came out with Ms. Pearl following close behind. She stopped within feet of the car. We rolled down the window to hear what they were saying.

Mrs. Elizabeth placed her hands on her hips, and got up close to Ms. Pearl's face. "You know why I am here, Pearl Brown. I want to know why you didn't let the people around here know it was Kindred you got killed and not Herman."

"I don't know what you are talking about."

"You know. My Kindred would never hang around a bar. Herman is the only man who couldn't live a decent life because you were his pride and joy. He was always following you to hell."

"I can't be out here listening to your accusations. I have a show to do tonight," Ms. Pearl said, and turned to walk away.

"You are a heartless women, Pearl Brown. You have managed to get three men killed. All of it is because of you. And you ain't worth much."

Ms. Pearl turned around and walked back up to Mrs. Elizabeth. "Kindred was not my type of man. He was too wimpy for me. He was in the wrong place. He was always coming around checking on Herman. He never let anybody know he was Herman's brother.

I think he liked pretending to be Herman to get away from you. At first I thought it was Herman who was murdered, but when he came to me and told me it was his brother, what did you want me to do?"

"I wish I had never let your ass in my house. When Herman brought you to visit us in D.C., I knew you would be nothing but trouble. The way you sashayed around like a floozy was too much. Look at you. Herman is gone and he thought you loved him. You don't even seem affected by his death."

"Why do you think he was down there with Mae Lou? I didn't want Herman Camm. He couldn't do anything for me. He didn't have any money and he was a damn fool. I told him to go back to Mae Lou; she was the only one that really loved him."

Pointing her finger, Mrs. Elizabeth said, "I want to tell you, you are a nasty woman. I hope you get what is coming to you."

"Elizabeth, go on back up to D.C. You've been sitting around waiting for Kindred for almost two years. Did it ever occur to you that he was not coming back home?"

When Ms. Pearl said those words, Mrs. Elizabeth drew her hand back and smacked Ms. Pearl so hard, a curl fell out of her hair. Ms. Pearl grabbed her face and backed up.

"Don't run." Mrs. Elizabeth stepped out of her high-heels. "I'm going to give you the whipping you deserve."

Ms. Pearl took off running and went back into the club. The guy at the door held back Mrs. Elizabeth, who was determined to go inside. Simon also ran after her.

Simon pulled her back and calmed her down. He picked up her shoes and helped her into the car. I had never seen a woman dressed so well break out into a brawl. She was determined to get Ms. Pearl.

We took Ms. Elizabeth home with us. We made a place for her on the davenport. On the way home, she ranted and raved about Ms. Pearl.

"Pearl Brown is someone no man needs to come across. She is selfish and loves attention. She doesn't care about anybody but herself. Two brothers dead and gone just because of her. She even had her own husband killed."

Simon cleared his throat. "Now, Ms. Elizabeth, you shouldn't say things like that."

"That floozy had that white man kill her own husband. Somebody told it to me."

"I wouldn't keep saying it," Simon warned her.

"Why are you taking up for her?"

"Because, she didn't force Herman or Kindred to come around her."

"Kindred did not come around her. He was mistaken for his good-for-nothing twin, Herman. I told him Herman was going to cost him his life, but he didn't listen. When Herman married Mae Lou, I thought he had turned from his wicked ways, but he hadn't. He was still a fool for Pearl Brown."

"You knew my momma?"

"He wrote us about her, said she was the best woman he ever did know. He told us how she went to church and all. That man thought the world of her, but Pearl has a way with the menfolk."

The conversation continued in the house once we were home.

"Did you know Ms. Pearl?"

"Yeah, I know her. She came to my house many times with Herman when her husband was overseas. She doesn't care about nothing and nobody."

"So, she was your friend?"

"Pearl ain't never been a friend of mine. I tolerated her for my husband's sake. He wanted Herman to feel welcomed in our home. Frankly, I could look at her and see she wasn't about much."

I went into the kitchen, poured her an ice-cold glass of milk and gave her a slice of the cake Momma had made.

"Thank you!" she said, and then continued, "Mae Lou told me what he did to you. She said he was sorry at the end."

"She told you?"

"Yes, she told me all those things knowing it was Herman in the casket and not my Kindred. I suppose they had talked quite a bit the last few months."

"So she believed him?"

"Your momma loved him," she said.

"I guess she did. For the life of me, I don't know why. He was a drunk."

"Now listen up, you don't know what a couple talks about when no one is around. He probably said all the right things." Mrs. Elizabeth gazed at the ceiling. "My Kindred could do things for me no other man in the world could do. I loved that man so much. Lawd, Lawd, Lawd!"

Simon had already gone to bed, had said our conversations were for women only.

"Ms. Elizabeth, you need to get some rest. The train leaves early in the morning."

Handing me the saucer, she said, "Take this into the kitchen. I'm going to go in the bathroom and put on my nightgown. Now you try to get some rest. You've had a long day too."

I crawled in the bed and slid close to Simon. I was exhausted. Tears streamed down my cheeks.

CHAPTER 24

I couldn't wait to get back to school. The drama of being home had been haunting. Every time I closed my eyes at night, I saw the white man holding a gun, and a dead man lying in the street. The flashbacks of Willie being shot also resurfaced. Then at times, I'd gaze out the window and watch Nadine and her two children sitting on the porch. Neither of those things made me happy. Simon said he was worried about me; he had caught me up at night, sitting in the dark. So, when it was time to go back to school, he drove me. I missed riding the train. The train had been the place where I did my thinking. I would close my eyes or gaze out the window at the livestock and the fields of tobacco. Occasionally, we would go past a corner feed-and-seed store. It was an excursion away from the things I could not get off my mind. I would envision taking a train ride to the beach or to another state. The shaking of the train never bothered me, and for an hour, I would lay my head back and relax.

Miriam was in the sitting room when I got to the boarding-house. She saw me when I came through the door and rushed over to me. She had her hair pulled back in a ponytail and was wearing a pleated skirt, cardigan and Friedman flappers. She knew how to coordinate her clothes. Some of us girls felt she was the best dressed on campus.

"I'm glad you're back. Adam has been over here every day in the last week looking for you. He sat right there in the parlor," Miriam said, pointing to the davenport. She continued, "He sat with me for over an hour talking about you. He really has missed you, Girl."

Instead of going straight upstairs to put down my bag, I walked into the parlor with her and sat down.

"Did he say what he needed?"

She tapped me on the arm as if she didn't have my attention already. "You know that boy is in love with you."

"We are friends, Miriam," I said.

She put her hand under her chin. "Well, I think he is in love with you. All he wanted to know was how you were doing in school and did I think you needed any help with anything. Seems to me he believes he has to look out for you."

I shook my head and smiled. "Miriam, you are making some of this up."

She giggled. "Well, the boy is into you."

I got up and she followed. "Did you get the homework for me?" I asked.

"You didn't miss anything, but I took notes anyhow."

We both went up the stairs. Once we were in our room, I began to unpack the few items I had in my suitcase. I hung up a dress and put all the small things in the drawer.

"I'm going to have to find you a fellow. You need someone to talk to while I am away," I said, smiling.

Miriam plopped down on the bed. She leaned back with her arms behind her head.

"I might already have someone."

"Who?" I asked, putting my underclothes in the drawer.

With a wide smile on her face, she giggled. She hesitated, as if she had to find the correct words. She picked up a book and put it back down. She finally glanced over at me, smiling.

"Well..." I said, and waited for her to talk.

"Adam introduced me to his cousin."

"Is he in school around here? I know he has relatives living in Petersburg."

"He lives around here. As a matter of fact, he spends a lot of time at the school."

I sat down on the bed. "Stop with the suspense; who is he?"

"He is one of the professors at school."

"At school, most of the men are old. Are you fooling around with someone old enough to be your daddy?" I asked, assuming he was old since most of the people at the school were twice our age. Adam was the youngest professor I knew at the school.

"Adam's cousin is working with him now in the history department. He came over here with him. Too bad you are married, because we could be going on double dates."

I listened to her go on and on about us double dating and even living in the same city. She was a hopeless romantic, who had only been out with the guy once. They had taken a walk one evening and he had promised they would have many dinners. She was attractive, and I could only imagine a cousin of Adam's having the same seriousness, kindness and dedication.

"Miriam, I don't know what to do."

"You know, you have got to be happy. Adam is a fine colored man. He is always saying the right things to you and about you. You shouldn't stay with Simon if he makes you unhappy," she said in a proper Southern drawl. It seemed to me that when things got to be serious, Miriam's manner and voice also changed.

"Simon wants me to understand. He was there for me when I had Robert."

"You don't owe him anything. What happened to you was not your fault. Robert is the outcome. Simon deliberately lied to you."

"I just don't know."

"If I was you, I'd leave him. He is not your type anyway. In a few years, you will have nothing in common with him."

I giggled. "I will always have the country in common with him."

"That will be it. Do you love him?" she asked, with her eyes squinted and her nose turned up.

"I used to love him with all my heart. Each lie has chipped away at my love for him."

"Seems like you are done with him; yet you are just hanging on because he helped you to leave Jefferson County. "

"No, that is not true. He used to be my best friend."

"Do that woman and her children still leave across the street?"

"They are there so he can keep a watch on the children."

"Girl, he's got a car; he can drive around the corner. He is a strange man. I thought he was busy working with the Colored League."

"I'm so confused, and there is no way I can mess up Adam's life right now."

"Do you care for Adam too?"

"Adam is so special to me. I just want to make sure things are right."

I could not commit to Adam or Simon. I had a lot of thinking to do. What I had experienced with Simon had me agitated, and vulnerable. Memories of my jaded past kept rising up inside me, and kept me in a tainted marriage. My plans were to dive into my books, and make the best grades in the normal school. I wanted to teach in

Richmond and help the young people to make better choices when it came to education. While I concentrated on my studies, I could only hope I would find a way to straighten out my life.

We had just finished talking when we were alerted of visitors in the parlor. Immediately, Miriam stood up in front of the mirror combing her hair in place and practicing the smile she would show Adam's cousin. I inhaled knowing I would have to say goodbye to Adam until I had things in order.

As we sat in the parlor with Adam and David, playing checkers, the entire room was filled with laughter. Miriam and David beat Simon and me four times. I had not laughed and had that much fun since I was a child. Just when everything was relaxed and we had played our last game of checkers, Adam asked to speak to me alone.

It was the beginning of the transition from spring to summer and the night air was warm and dry and the sky dark except for the sparkles of the stars. It was a perfect night to spend with someone you loved.

We sat down on the porch glider and searched for the North Star.

"Isn't it fascinating how the slaves had the wisdom to follow the North Star to Canada?" Adam said, and pulled my hand into his. I was uncomfortable at first, but soon was enjoying the way it felt to be shown affection. I quickly forgot about being married.

Adam put his arm around me and kissed me on the lips. "I've been concerned about you ever since the shootings at the club. When I walked you home, I hated to leave you there alone."

"I think being here is good for me. I don't think about the club or anything else. I get to concentrate on completing my studies."

"Do you want to be with me, Carrie?" he asked.

I peered up at the sky and found the brightest star and focused on it. Then I answered, "I do, but I can't see you anymore, Adam.

I've got to figure my life out. I don't want you in my mess."

"We are not just getting to know each other; we have history, Carrie. You can't just throw it all away."

I tightened my grip on his hand. "I want to be sure about us. I can't have you waiting for me while I wait for Simon. I want things to be done right."

He shook his head. "It is simple; leave him."

"It's not as simple as you say."

"What do you want to do?" he asked louder, more sternly.

"I want you to go on with your life. If we are meant to be, we will find our way back together."

"I am here with you. I took this job to be close to you. Now, you want to push me away."

"I want us to have the best possible start. I need you to understand," I said, gazing at the stars. When I glanced at Adam, he had tears in his eyes. When I noticed it, my eyes welled up and the teardrops slid down my cheeks.

"No matter what, I know we will be together," he said.

"I know we will too," I mumbled.

He got up from the glider and pulled me up too. He held me close in his arms. I put my head on him and the tears poured like the rain. He wiped them and kissed me intensely on the lips. I could feel him all over my body. I wanted to say yes, but I didn't. I pulled back from him. He shook his head.

"I know you've got some decisions to make. Just keep focused on the schoolwork, and pray the rest of our lives will fall into place," he said, and walked away.

He was so soothing to me. He said the things I needed to hear. Now, I needed to do what was right and either reconcile with Simon, or be alone.

CHAPTER 25

"I need you to accept my children," Simon said, as if I had rejected his children. I actually liked how his daughter had handled herself the day I went to visit Nadine. She was tired of lying and wanted to make sure the truth was told. The little girl ignored her momma's demand, and was bold and courageous enough to say something about a subject it was obvious she'd been told to keep to herself.

"I already accept your children," I assured him.

"They want to come over here and play with Robert," he said.

"Simon, I don't think that is a good idea. Your children are too old to play with Robert. He is just a little boy."

"I think they should know each other. Besides, we are family."

I couldn't believe he was asking me to take his children in. The next thing he'd want me to do would be to let Nadine drop by whenever she wanted. I stood my ground and stared him in the eyes. "Do you really think I want Nadine coming over here?"

"Nadine is not coming, just the children."

I felt like a thirty-year-old woman in a teenager's body. I had been forced to grow up too fast, and because of it, I acted more like an adult than my peers. I had a baby of my own I didn't spend enough time with, and now he wanted me to take on the children of his mistress. Who did he think I was? Did he really know anything about me? At times I felt I didn't know him. He had lied about the children, and now, without thinking, he was asking me to become a mother again. The last thing I wanted to share was my living space with his other family.

"I can't do it, Simon. It is bad enough I have to see them every day when I come and go in my own home. They are across the street."

"Grow up, Carrie. You know about the children. I have told you everything. My daughter wants to get to know her little brother. Is that so bad?"

I stormed out of the kitchen, and Simon followed. "Simon, do whatever you feel. Just don't think I am going to take care of them."

"Carrie, you are selfish. You don't want any more children. You don't even want to take care of Robert, and now you are trying to deny my children from visiting their daddy. I'm their daddy, Carrie."

"You said they wanted to visit Robert; now you want them here with you. They live across the street, not around the way some-where. I'm not selfish. I am still young, Simon. I shouldn't have to take on everybody's mess."

"Just let them come over today. Nadine is going to look for a job."

I knew it was about Nadine. Whatever Nadine wanted, she got.

"So, why did you even ask?"

Shortly after our conversation, the two children knocked on the door. Simon opened the door and let them in. Neither of the children spoke to me, and the little girl rolled her eyes up in her head and stared at me as if she was in charge and a grown woman.

"Y'all hungry?" I asked them. Still, neither of them said any-thing.

Simon went over to the stove. "We've got some fried chicken if you want some."

"I do, Daddy," the little boy said, and I cringed.

I went over to the stove and got a biscuit and a chicken leg and put it on a plate. I set the plate on the table. The children still didn't say anything.

"Thank you," I said. "You should tell me thank you."

"You are not our mother," the little girl argued.

I waited for Simon to say something to them, but he didn't. He just smiled and accommodated them. He put their food on plates, and set the plates on the kitchen table. Then he told the girl, who had been rolling her eyes at me, and the boy, to sit down. Robert had been playing on the floor. He stared at them, pulled up, and trotted over to them.

"Don't come over here, baby," the little boy said. "My momma said you are not our brother; you are an ole man's child."

What he said caused my blood to boil. I cut my eyes over at him.

"Be quiet now," Simon warned him, but it was too late. Now I knew Nadine knew about Robert, and the only way she could have known was from Simon.

"He is your brother," I said, "and Simon is his daddy too."

"Momma said he ain't," he said again.

"Be quiet, little Simon. I'm gonna tell Momma on you," the little girl threatened. I watched her glance over at her brother in an attempt to keep him quiet.

"But, she said it," little Simon shot back.

Simon was without words. He sat there grinning and seemingly clueless about how to keep him quiet. The girl nudged her dad, and put her finger over her lip. "Be quiet!" she yelled.

Little Simon's eyes suddenly were wide open. He tucked his little head and whispered, "Momma said it."

I stood beside the stove waiting for Simon to say something to the little boy, yet he didn't open his mouth. It occurred to me that the little boy was the most honest person in the room. Momma had always said children would tell the truth if adults did not insist on them lying to save face. The little girl had already learned how to keep secrets. I looked down at Robert, who was holding on to my legs, and wondered what secrets of mine he'd be forced to keep. I decided at the moment to never force a child to lie for me. Why must they carry such a load?

After the children had eaten, they came into the sitting room and sat on the floor with Robert and played with the blocks. Simon didn't say anything at all; he sat in the high-back chair admiring the family he had created.

It wasn't long before Nadine knocked on the door. I beat Simon to the door.

"I came to pick up my children," she said, with a smirk on her face, as if to say, '*I have won this battle.*' I saw it and for the first time, I didn't care.

"Your mom is here!" I yelled to them.

Nadine asked, "Can I come in?"

"No, you can't," I said, and stood at the door until the children came. Then I waited there until Nadine and her children started down the stairs. I slammed the door.

Again, Simon had let me down. I spent the rest of the day cleaning the house, restoring it to the organized state it was in prior to me going to school. It didn't take much. I also fed the chickens out back that Mr. Hall had been caring for while I'd been away. It was like something inside of me was propelling me to move. It was as if I'd been in an undisturbed world and now I had intruders vowing to take over. When I was done, I put Robert down for a nap, and sat down in the parlor, pulled out my school-work and attempted to focus on all the things I enjoyed doing.

Simon was about to leave when someone knocked hard on the door. Simon beat me to the door. When he opened the door, I heard him shout, "What's happening?! What's going on?!"

I got up to go see what was going on, and there was a policeman holding Simon down with his knee in his back.

"What are y'all doing?" I asked. Simon was peering back at me, but he didn't seem afraid.

One of the policeman said, "Your husband is under arrest for the murder of Herman Camm."

My jaw dropped. Simon said, "Carrie, go let Ms. Pearl know what is going on. Tell her to get me out."

I shook my head yes. As they coaxed him down the stairs toward the paddy wagon, I noticed Nadine standing on her porch. She had her hand over her mouth.

"What is going on?!" she yelled.

The Halls were also sitting on their porch.

I watched as she pranced around as if he was her man. When the wagon pulled off, she came across the street swinging her arms and practically ran up the stairs. "Carrie, what is going on?"

I inhaled to gain my composure; then I gazed her into her eyes. "Nadine, it is none of your business."

"Why you feel that way? He is my children's daddy."

"Like I said, it is none of your business. Now get off my steps before I push you down them."

She turned and took off down the stairs. I went inside, picked up my books, and continued with my schoolwork. I was not going to let Simon worry me. I would stop by to see Ms. Pearl when I felt like it. It was about time for Simon to slow down, give himself some time to think.

CHAPTER 26

I didn't run straight to Ms. Pearl with the news of Simon's arrest. I stopped by to see her on my way back to school. I would have completely missed her had I been able to drive Simon's car. I would have driven it to Petersburg, and taken the street that bypassed the club. I did stop by on Monday afternoon on the way to school. I asked the bouncer standing at the door if he could ask Ms. Pearl to step outside for a minute. I didn't want to step foot in the place. It was dangerous as long as Pearl Brown was the entertainment.

Ms. Pearl walked out the door looking around as if she expected something to happen. "What is going on, Carrie?" she asked after noticing me standing and waiting. She was dressed in a low-waist show dress, her hair perfect and the matte powder covering up any flaws on her face.

As I waited for her, I had already scanned my surroundings for anything suspicious. The club was notorious for violence. It was a warm day and the atmosphere calm. Folks were strolling down the street with smiles on their faces, enjoying the sun.

"Simon has been arrested, Ms. Pearl. He told me to let you know."

"What was he arrested for?"

"They said he murdered Herman Camm. They picked him up on Saturday."

She bit her bottom lip, and shook her head. "Okay, let me handle this. I will do what I can for Simon."

"Yes, Ma'am," I answered. I was clueless about what she could do for him. I was afraid to ask.

She tapped me on the shoulder as if to console me. "Now don't worry about him; he can handle himself. I will get somebody on it immediately."

"Yes, Ma'am," I said, and walked away. I headed straight to the train station. I had no doubts she could handle what was going on with Simon. She seemed to be as dangerous as any man and she was afraid of no one.

When I got to Petersburg, I was unprepared for what awaited me. When I got off the train, Adam was waiting. "What are you doing here?" I asked him.

"I knew you were coming back today, so I decided to come and meet you."

He was wearing a pair of cuffed trousers and a white button-down shirt. He grabbed my suitcase.

"Adam, you can't keep doing this. It is hard enough without you popping up from time to time."

He listened to me, but I could tell he was going to do what he felt was right. Adam knew I loved him. I wasn't sure if we would ever be a couple, because now all I wanted to do was work on getting over Simon.

"You should be happy somebody cares enough to want to take care of you. It is difficult to do what you are doing and raise a child. You are special to me, and I will always feel like I need to take care of you. Do you remember when we first met?" he asked as we walked to the boardinghouse.

"Of course, I remember," I said, smiling from ear to ear. "You showed me all the steps needed to get into school and even went with me to enroll. Adam, you are the nicest and smartest man I know."

"If that is true, then why are you trying to run me away?"

We turned down the street toward the boardinghouse. "I don't want to be confused anymore. I don't want to love you because I need someone in my life. I want to love you because I love you. And, I can't do it if I'm confused and torn."

"I understand," he said, although his face reflected something different.

"I hope so, because I never want to lose you as my friend," I said and reached out and touched his face. He smiled. "Don't take too long, okay?"

He carried my luggage up the steps to the front door of the boardinghouse and set it on the porch. He turned and went back down the steps and waved. I watched him walk down the street and merge into the trees. It was the first time since I had known him that he didn't kiss me at least on the cheek goodbye. I was all of a sudden vulnerable.

I picked up my bag and went inside and up the stairs toward my room. I paused before entering and wiped the tears creeping out the side of my eyes. Adam was more special than I could admit. Now I was faced with a deep sense of desperation to do something soon.

Miriam filled my ears with the excitement of dating. I listened, but not with my entire heart. My mind was on Adam and the things I had to get straight.

I spent the entire summer in Petersburg. I ran from school to the boardinghouse. I had asked for more work hours so I could pay the bills in Richmond. I found out when I had asked the Halls whom I needed to contact to pay the rent, that Simon owned our building. The information was shocking. It was yet another thing I didn't know about my husband.

So, I worked very hard to get the best grades I could. I studied in all of my free time until Miriam convinced me to go with her to a place the students got sandwiches and listened to music.

Adam was there with a beautiful young lady, her hair hanging down her back like an Indian. She looked exactly like the woman I expected him to be with. I had assumed he was into the attractive and classy type. I wasn't sure if I fit the description anymore. He saw me and walked over to the table. I had not seen him in two months.

"How are you, Carrie?" he asked, studying me with his serious, dark eyes.

"I'm fine," I replied, smiling. I missed seeing him even if it had been at my request. The woman he was with stood across the room watching him.

David and Miriam were cuddled together gazing into each other's eyes. It was beautiful to see couples admire one another. Simon and I had been like that. I thought about him daily, but more in a sympathetic way.

"You are looking fine," I said to Adam.

"You've lost weight," he replied with concerned eyes. I had lost weight. I had been working so hard, I could only get in one meal a day. I got up early, worked in the kitchen preparing breakfast for the tenants in the boardinghouse. Afterward, I would go to school and help one my professors clean the laboratory. She paid me out of her own pocket. I was determined to stash money away for Robert and me. I didn't know what might happen once Simon was released.

"Adam, I am a little thinner. I have been too busy to eat."

"Just take care of yourself," he commented, and walked away.

He grabbed the girl he was with by the hand and escorted her out of the café.

Miriam tapped me on the arm. "Stop staring."

"I didn't know I was staring."

"You are. See, you shouldn't have pushed him away."

"Who is she?" I wanted to know.

"She is a friend. They just started dating. You know he is such a gentleman."

I was absorbed by what I had just witnessed. I didn't know it would be an issue, but it was.

CHAPTER 27

The leaves had turned yellow, orange and red. It was a colorful sight, and a beautiful introduction to fall. Simon was still in jail when I came home the first week of September. Ms. Pearl had promised to get him released, yet for some reason, he was still in the county jail. Mrs. Hall had been to visit him twice. She said he was like family to her.

"He wants you to come to see him," she said, when I stopped by to get Robert for the weekend. I held my hands out to Robert, so I could pick him up, and he acted like he didn't know me. When I picked him up, he kicked and screamed until I gave in, and put him back down. He no longer knew me; the frequent trips to school and then staying in Petersburg for the last two months had taken a toll on our relationship.

"Do you remember me?" I asked Robert, and he ran over to Mrs. Hall and stayed there.

"He will take to you as soon as you get him home," she assured me after seeing the disappointment in my face.

"Mrs. Hall, has Robert been too much for you?" I asked her.

"To be honest, we miss him when he goes upstairs with you. We love having a child to care for and he loves being with us. I feel like he is my child. I hope you will not get angry, but if we could keep him permanently, we would. He is a joy for the both of us."

I knew I was not the best mother, and even though I thought about my child every day, my finishing school was the most important thing for our future. Though I admitted I enjoyed the freedom associated with being able to come and go whenever I chose. One of the girls at school had a baby and she was always late for class, and as soon as her day ended on campus, it was just beginning at home. She could never spend time after class with her friends, and the teachers were threatening to fail her. I had a baby, too, yet I had the Halls. I knew God was watching over me.

"Mrs. Hall, I was adopted, and although I had a great childhood, I can't see signing him over to you at this time. I couldn't live with him thinking I didn't love him."

"Listen, Child, you don't need to think about that. Just know we are here for you and we love him as if he was our own."

Mr. Hall had been quiet, and most times it was difficult to get him to talk, yet he had to add something to our conversation.

"Carrie, the boy needs a man in his life. I am here for him and I can teach him things."

Tears welled up in my eyes. "You both have been good to both of us. I am so glad you all love my son. When I think of Robert being here, I am never worried. You all are the best family anybody could have."

Mrs. Hall got a few of Robert's toys and put them in a bag. "Now bring these back with Robert. I am teaching him his ABCs."

"He is just one."

"It is never too early to teach him and now is a good time to start."

I sat down on the davenport. "I don't know what to do, Mrs. Hall."

She sat back down. "Just go and visit Simon. You don't have to commit to anything. Now may be a good time to start something brand-new."

Mrs. Hall was flawless in most ways. She lived her life with coloreds and I had never heard a mumble of regret. She adored her husband, and she was the twinkle in his eye. When I thought about loving someone, I often thought about how they interacted. Mr. Hall was the gentleman most women admired and she was his princess. I thought I was Simon's princess. The way he saved me from the whispers of Jefferson County made me feel like a queen. Those thoughts had slowly dissolved, and now they were floating further out in the sea. I didn't love him like a husband any longer.

"I'll go to see him in the morning, Mrs. Hall. I'll drop Robert down on my way out."

"Well, you don't need to take all of his things upstairs if that's the case."

"Okay. I will just take him and try to get to know him again," I said, smiling and feeling like a mother who had abandoned her child.

I picked Robert up and he started to squirm out of my arms. I held onto him until he settled down; then we left. He cried at least twenty minutes after we were in the apartment. The only way I could get him to be quiet was by bribing him with a piece of sweet bread Mrs. Hall had sent home for him.

After fighting with Robert, I was tired. I gave him a bath. He lay down beside me and cried his little self to sleep. I gazed at him and examined his small features. He was changing. He no longer looked exactly like me. Now, he had some of his father's features, the small beady eyes and long slender hands. It bothered me, and a chill traveled throughout my body. I knew it would not be long before he would take on some of his father's features. So far, for the most part, he favored me. I knew Herman would live on through Robert and felt I could deal with it.

I finally dozed off to sleep thinking about the things I had endured. I was especially grateful for having a family like the Halls in my life.

I woke up early the next morning, bathed and fixed Robert some oats for breakfast. He woke up looking around for Mrs. Hall. He began to whine, but quickly changed his mind when I began to feed him his breakfast.

I took Robert with me to the backyard to get the eggs from the hens and to feed them. It was something he enjoyed doing with Mr. Hall; I was determined to make Robert smile. He loved the chickens; Mrs. Hall had often said so. Now, I was able to see for myself. He trotted across the yard and I ran after him. He giggled. He was a happy baby.

After putting away the eggs, I took Robert downstairs. He saw the Halls and squirmed until I put him on the floor. He ran to Mrs. Hall and grabbed the tail of her dress. Mr. Hall held his arms out for him and Robert ran straight to him.

"I'm going down to the jail," I said.

"You shouldn't have any trouble seeing him."

I walked over to Mr. Hall who was holding Robert. "Give me a hug, little boy," I said, smiling. Robert grinned and leaned over and kissed me. My heart filled with joy.

I left the house not knowing what I might find. I had not seen Simon since the day his children had come over for a visit. It was also the day I'd found out the children knew more about me than I did about them.

It was warmer than usual for a fall day, and as I walked south down Broad Street toward the jail, I could feel the beads of sweat trickling down my face. I usually didn't perspire much, but along with the heat, my nerves were rattled. I found every reason to turn around and go back home, but I couldn't. I forged through my nerves and the sun. When I got to the entrance of the jail, I inhaled to gain the courage to go inside a place nobody wanted to be in or visit.

I sat directly across from Simon. His eyes glistened with joy and a wide smile appeared on his face. I felt very uncomfortable there. It was the place most colored folks feared on a daily basis. It was a boring, unattractive place that was airy and chilly. The walls were cement and a small window no larger than the size of a book appeared to be the only sunlight entering the place.

"I knew you would come," he said, wearing a black-and-white-striped jumpsuit.

"You okay?" I asked him, knowing it was impossible to be okay in a place like that.

He smiled. "I am now. You are here."

"I almost didn't make it. I don't like this place."

"Nobody likes it," he said.

"I know. I am so sorry you are here," I said, glancing around at the damp walls and drafty room with a musty stench.

I got right to the point. "Did you kill Herman Camm?"

"Why do you ask that?" Simon said, with his hands clasped together while he twirled his thumbs in a circular motion.

Simon had many telltale signs whenever he was upset, nervous or concerned. Twirling his thumbs indicated to me he was still trying to figure things out. I could tell there were things he couldn't talk about. And now I knew some things were better left unsaid.

"What are you going to do? Did Ms. Pearl come to see about you?"

"No, but she sent somebody down here to talk to me. They are trying to get me released soon. Can we talk about us?" he asked, determined to keep things to himself.

"There's not much to talk about."

"I've been in here almost three full months. It may be two months...I forget the time. This is the first time you've visited me. Why haven't you been to see me?"

"I had a lot of things to work out."

"What things?"

"Your children, Nadine, school, our marriage...a whole lot..."

Shaking his head, he asked, "Did you come up with a decision of sorts? You are my wife, and you ought to care what happens to me."

"I do care. I just didn't want to come up here without thinking things through."

"Did you ever think I might need something while I'm stuck in this filthy place?"

"I don't know anything about jail—only the things I've heard. Well, I know, but..."

"How are the children doing?" he interrupted.

"Robert is fine."

"How about the children across the street? Have you seen them?"

"I don't know. I've been away at school. I still can't believe your family is across the street. Has Nadine been to visit you?"

"She came up here a couple of times."

"I hope she gave you a good report," I said facetiously.

He adjusted himself in the metal chair, and moved in closer. "I am sorry about not telling you about my children."

I shook my head. "Knowing they had been living across the street for over a year and I never knew they were your children is unbelievable."

"I'm sorry. I plan on getting out of here soon and making it up to you."

"The damage is already done. When you sent for me, I was trying to escape all the things that were happening around me.

You were my knight, Simon. I was living in a bad place. I really hated myself. I feel I've had to deal with some of life's biggest shocks in such a short time. I've had to grow up fast. I didn't do anything to bring this all on myself. I loved you, Simon. At least, I thought I did."

"Carrie, I love you. But I live a different life than what you know."

"You have a lot of secrets. I am too young to have to worry so much."

"My life is a little complicated right now."

"I thought you wanted to be like Pete Hill and the other great colored players."

"I still do," he said with sad eyes.

"You were friends with my brothers. None of us really knew you."

"When you met me, I was playing ball, but I met some people who offered me ways to make some real money."

I shook my head. "You know being caught up with white people can get you killed. The ones in the club are not like Mrs. Hall. They are different. How could you do this?"

"I didn't mean to hurt you. I thought I was giving you and your baby a better life."

I forced a smile. "My baby…"

"I can't live like they do in the country. I need to be able to enjoy things. Think about it. Have you ever had to worry about money since you married me?"

"Now I worry about everything," I shot back.

"Your time is almost up," the sheriff in the room said.

"Simon, who pays the bills now?"

"If you had come to see me, you'd know I have cash in the cigar box under the bed. It is enough money to pay for food, anything, for a few years."

"When are you getting out of here?"

"I only have three more months to serve. But right now, I need you to do something for me." I listened to him talk, but for some reason, it didn't feel like my husband. It was like I had been talking to a stranger. He was not the handsome, kind man I knew. He had changed into someone I couldn't understand.

"What do you need from me?"

"Take a hundred dollars out of the box, and give it to Nadine. Listen up, this is for the children."

"Sure," I said.

"I need you, Carrie. You are a strong, good person. I can tell you are going to try to leave me."

"You will be all right, Simon," I commented as the tears welled up in my eyes.

"Tell Ms. Hall, I could use some of that cornbread and cake she brought up here," he said, grinning as if he didn't have a care in the world.

"I will tell her. But you never answered my question. Did you do it?"

"Carrie, I will tell you everything when I am out of here."

I inhaled. "Simon, I won't be waiting for you when you get out."

"Now, don't go acting crazy. I am the Simon you used to know. Things are just too complicated right now. They will get better."

"I agree with you; it is too confusing. I just can't deal with it," I said, standing up.

"Carrie, come back to see me."

"Maybe I will. I really don't know," I commented, feeling disappointed and scared for him.

His facial expression changed, as if a storm cloud had passed over us. I could see the veins jumping in his neck. Then he sang out, "I loved you, Girl. You ain't gonna be happy with that soft country boy."

"I'm by myself, Simon. The way you left me."

I watched him swallow, and gain control. "I'm sorry, Carrie."

"I'll be okay, Simon," I mumbled, "I just want you to take care of yourself." I struggled to fight back tears.

"I'm all right, I told you." He raised his voice. The sheriff came over and pulled him by the arm to leave. He pulled away. "Get yo' hands off me." He stood straight up.

He blew me a kiss when I got up to leave. I forced a grin. I could tell he was not afraid. He had sold his soul to the white man. He knew he would take care of him.

CHAPTER 28

I had no trouble getting a divorce from Simon. I went straight to the courthouse on Broad Street and filled out the papers. Once I told the white lady working there that my husband was in jail, she quickly took a seat beside me and assisted me in filling out the papers. "Now don't say I told you this, but no woman needs a man who is always getting himself in trouble. Don't take this the wrong way, but you colored girls ought to stand up for yourselves. I'm going to make sure these papers are filed today."

I had sleepless nights after visiting Simon. I wondered if leaving him was truly the answer to our problems, or should I have regurgitated our wedding vows once more, and let them stick close to my heart. I had vowed to stay through good and bad times. I couldn't do it. I was too young to be miserable any longer. Ever since I was fifteen years old, I'd had to deal with something. First, my papa died, and then Mr. Camm came, then Robert, and now Simon. It was time I did some things to help me find my way. I cried at the first sight of the divorce decree, and then I smiled. Now, I was free to make my own choices.

The divorce papers were kept in my pocketbook. For some reason, I needed the security of knowing they were close by. I had just read through the document thoroughly when someone knocked on the door. Hester had been my last caller, and she only stayed an hour. Now, who could this be?

When I opened the door, Nadine was there. "What do you want?" I asked.

"Can I come in?"

I couldn't let her in. "No, you can't come in. Go home, Nadine, and leave me alone."

"Please let me in, Carrie. I really need to talk to you," she begged.

I was about to shut the door in her face when all of a sudden, something told me to let her in. I opened the door and she came in. It was the first time she'd been in the apartment that she wasn't looking around for Simon.

"Can I sit down, please?"

I took a deep breath, paused, and said, "Yes."

Nadine pulled out a seat at my kitchen table. I sat down too.

"Why are you over here, Nadine?" I asked, studying her from top to bottom.

"I wanted to tell you the truth."

I turned up my lips, and rolled my eyes. There was no way she wanted to tell the truth. It was the money she wanted, and I already knew it.

Before I could say anything, she started, "The children and I have been having a hard time since their father was put in jail. He used to take care of them."

"Is it the truth you came over here to tell?" I asked, knowing she was not being transparent.

"I wanted you to know we didn't mean you no harm."

"You really need to tell me why you are here. I don't have time to play around with you. I have someplace to go," I said, after glancing at the clock on the wall.

"I went to see Simon today and he said you were going to bring some money over for the kids."

Before she could finish, I asked her, "Do you make a habit of visiting other women's husbands in jail?"

"Me and Simon been friends since we were children. He is my best friend."

"Nadine, tell the truth. You and Simon have been doing things behind my back for a long time."

She looked away to gather her thoughts. "I had a man who used to live with me. He was good to me."

"Nadine, you need to leave. I'm not going to sit here and listen to any more lies. You can go back across the street," I said, and got up from the table. She reached over and grabbed my arm. "Please let me explain."

I pulled my arm away from her and sat back down. I wanted to hear the truth explained in detail.

"We have had an on-and-off relationship for eight years. He was my first love. He has been real good to us. He bought the house we live in and he gave me money for food each month. When he met you, we stopped being together like that. We just talked about the children."

I peered at her across the table. "I don't believe you."

"I'm telling the truth," she said, massaging her fingers through her thick, coarse hair.

"You and Simon have been together. I caught you in my house." With the release of the word "house," I started to get angry.

"I was only with him twice since you've been here."

"You don't care about anything, do you? We are married." I didn't dare let her in on my truth—that I was no longer married to him.

"I just didn't want him to leave me and the children," she said, pleading.

"Are they really his children, Nadine? Do you even know? I suspect your daughter is his, but the little boy looks nothing like him."

"Simon is good. He accepts him just like he does your Robert."

When she said "Robert," I jumped up and moved in on her. She put her hands over her face. "Please don't hit me."

"Did Simon tell you all my business?"

"All he said was that he was going to take care of Robert just as he had done for little Simon."

"So, he knows Simon is not his child?"

"I told him the truth one day. I wanted him to be Simon's; that is why I named my son after him. My daughter is his."

"You are a low-down liar. You don't care, do you?" Nadine didn't move, but kept looking at me with fear in her eyes.

Nadine became fidgety and tears spilled down her face. "I'm sorry. I just wanted him for me and the children. He takes care of us. My son's father doesn't even come around."

"What is the real reason you stopped by?"

"Simon said you had some money over here for me and the kids. We don't have any food in the house. Can you help us?"

The devil in me wanted to send her home without anything, but I could never mistreat the children. "You stay here," I said and went into my bedroom, pulled out the box and took some cash out to give her. I gave her a little more than Simon said to give, since I had found a chest full of money in the back of the closet. And, I didn't want her making a habit of coming to me for money.

"Thank you for helping me and my children. I am so sorry for all I've done to you."

"Why did you sleep with my husband? You knew he was married to me," I said, and waited.

"I wanted him for me. He is the only man I've ever loved. He will always be the man I love, but he belongs to you now."

I opened the door. "Go get your children some food."

She faked a smile. "Can they visit Robert from time to time?"

"Maybe..."

I shut the door.

CHAPTER 29

The musty stench of the jail lingered in my nostrils long after I had inhaled the freshness of the air outdoors. The dankness remained after I had turned the corner and left the place that Simon now called home. Simon seemed good despite being in jail. He appeared healthy and seemed to have put on a few additional pounds of muscle. I told him about the money I had found in the closet. All he said was, "Use it if you have to; just save me a little for when I get out of this place." He thought he would be released soon, but Ms. Pearl had confirmed he would be released in late winter or early spring; she said it had taken longer than usual to get him out.

"Are you worried about getting out of this place?" I asked him, looking around at the mundane green paint on the walls and watching the cockroach creep around on the ceiling. He didn't seem to mind.

"Don't nobody stay in the can for killing a deadbeat like Camm. I will be out in by the spring," he confirmed.

I asked him what he needed and informed him I would be moving out when he was released.

"I expected you to get a divorce, and eventually leave me. I want you to know I really did love you."

I frowned. "Believe it or not, Nadine is expecting y'all to get back together. She told me all about y'all."

He ignored my comment. "Carrie, I will do anything to help you. Take some of my money with you to school. Buy yourself some clothes, whatever you need."

"I don't want anything, Simon."

"Isn't there something you want to tell me?" he asked.

"What are you talking about? Whatever Nadine has told you about me is a lie. She knows way too much about me anyway."

"Why you didn't tell me about the divorce?"

I was shocked he knew, since I had not told anyone. I had planned on telling him once he was out of jail and free from all of the craziness.

I paused. "How did you find out?"

"The clerk sent word to me. Didn't you think I needed to know?"

"I was going to tell you, Simon, I really was. I just didn't want to upset you while you were in here."

"I know you, Carrie. You are too nice and you care too much about people. I couldn't tell you about all the things I did. You wouldn't have understood. I function in a different world than you do. My friends are not good people. But I will always be here for you." And then he gazed directly into my eyes. "You are still as innocent as the first day I met you on the farm in Jefferson County. I never wanted you to wait for me, but I wish you would have told me about the divorce. That bothers me, Carrie," he said solemnly, as if I had broken his heart.

"I didn't want to hurt you. I didn't want to leave you after all we've been through. I'm going to move out of the apartment as soon as I can," I said, before he could go on.

"You stay there with Robert. I can't do anything with it from here; plus I told you I will always take care of you. There is plenty of money for the two of you."

I became agitated. "Simon, how many women do you take care of? Nadine says you pay her bills too. She is one of the reasons I divorced you."

He shook his head. "She is my children's mother and I am never going to turn my back on my children."

"Well, that is why we can't be together. I find it difficult to share."

I got up to leave.

"You never had to share. You just aren't cut out for my lifestyle. One of these days you might come back to me. When you do, I will be waiting."

I thought about Simon all the way to the train station. Several times, I stopped to turn around and go back to the jailhouse. I didn't know what I was going to say, but I felt awful for divorcing him without notice. What could he have done anyway? I thought.

Before I left, Robert whimpered when I dropped him off at the Halls. Mrs. Hall kissed him and quieted him down, and then she warned me that it wouldn't be easy to say goodbye to Simon, either. She was right. He was still my knight in shining armor and seemingly, Nadine's too.

When I sat down, put my head back, and closed my eyes on the train, Nadine's old man tapped me on the shoulder. "I heard about Simon," he said. "I'm glad he is where he belongs. You are too good of a girl for him."

I forced a grin. "What did he do to you?"

"He was messing around with my lady. He kept coming over there, handing her money."

I nodded. "Oh, okay," I mumbled. For some reason, I was numb. What he said did not bother me at all. I assumed telling me was a way for him to move forward.

Before he walked away, he said, "If you need anyone to talk to, I'll be right here."

I nodded, and closed my eyes.

It amazed me how the summer and fall had come and gone and now the branches were bare again, the wind swirling as if snow was not far away. I had witnessed yet another murder, and perhaps my husband had been the one who did it, yet he would not say. I learned I had two stepchildren and had gotten a divorce, all in less than a year.

I had not seen Adam since our encounter at the sandwich shop. I was certain he had moved on with his life. The girl he was with seemed to have his attention. I was sure he was not thinking about me anymore. After all, I couldn't involve him in my problems. Time had a way of helping to sort out the troubles and kinks in life. I had taken more than enough time.

All sorts of thoughts came into my mind as I walked toward the boardinghouse. When I opened the door to the house, Miriam, David and Adam were leaving. They were giggling and acting like teenagers. "You're back," Adam said. He was dressed in a wool scarf and coat and Miriam had a cloak around her shoulders. It was chilly. He grabbed my bag from my hand and headed up the stairs to our room.

Miriam stood on the stairs smiling. "We were just talking about you. You have a lot of work to catch up on."

"I've only been away a week."

"It is finals, and we have a lot of homework."

I had been reading every night. It had been a soothing way to take my mind off what was going on around me. I was certain I was on top of things at school.

"I've been studying," I said, and started up the stairs.

"I put your bag at the door," Adam said, coming down the stairs.

I had taken deliberate steps to avoid him at school. I'd go around the building and come in the side entrance to avoid going past the classroom he usually taught in. I knew his schedule and had figured out ways to make myself scarce. Seeing him in front of me on the stairs brought back all the happy thoughts of my times with Adam. And it was hard to keep from smiling at the sight of him.

"You seem happy," Adam said, grinning from ear to ear.

"I am," I said, returning the gesture.

"Why don't you go with us to the sandwich shop? We thought we'd get a bite to eat before nightfall."

"Are you all meeting anyone else?"

Before anyone else could answer, Miriam said, "No, it is just the three of us, and if you come, it will be four. We are celebrating the end of the term."

"It is not over yet. I'll be right back," I said, going up the stairs. I went into the bathroom and freshened up. I brushed my teeth and patted my hair in place. Then I came back down the stairs. All three of them were sitting in the parlor watching the sparks from the wood burning in the fireplace float in the air and fall as ash.

Miriam glanced over at David. "It is so romantic down here."

David was quiet. He reached over and grabbed her hand. I sat down beside them and gazed at the burning wood too. Adam sat in the chair in front of me.

"I'm so glad to see you," he said. "It has been months since we've seen each other."

"I know," I said, staring into the fire.

Miriam said, "You know, we could have something to eat here. I made a cranberry loaf the other night. It is in the icebox." She got up from the davenport and went in the kitchen. I followed right behind her. I made black tea with honey and Miriam warmed up the bread in the oven before slicing it. After we put everything together, we invited the men into the kitchen.

The loaf and tea was a perfect way to warm up on a chilly winter's night. We gathered around the table. We discussed the people on campus and the changes at the school until it was nightfall. Out of nowhere, Adam said to me, "You look different, like you don't have a care in the world."

"I don't."

Miriam commented, "You have a husband and a child. There is no way you don't have stress."

"I guess now is a good time to tell you all. I am divorced."

A smile rolled across Adam's face. "Are you okay with it?"

"I'm happy," I said and took a sip of the tea. Miriam smiled.

After we had finished eating, all four of us decided to take a stroll. We put on our coats and walked from the boardinghouse to the campus of the normal school and back. Adam held my hand so tight it was numb.

When we came back inside from the bitterness of the winter chill, he said, "I've been waiting a long time for you." He pulled me close to him and kissed me passionately. I could feel the warmth travel all throughout my body.

READER'S DISCUSSION GUIDE

1. Why is Nadine so determined to get the attention of Simon?

2. Mae Lou came to check on Carrie; do you feel she had other motives?

3. It is the 1920s, why is it important to have Mrs. Hall in the story?

4. Carrie is growing up and she is taking on a new persona throughout the story. What makes Carrie's journey so interesting?

5. Kindred Camm has not done anything at all, yet people are worried about him. Is he an honest threat to the Jackson Heights community?

6. Pearl Brown has not changed much. Her soul has been sold for her career; is there relevance to this today?

7. Simon has changed since his introduction in *Blackberry Days of Summer*. Is he still the man Carrie fell in love with?

8. The white man remains a mystery throughout the story. What part does he really play in the life of Pearl?

9. Do you feel Carrie really loves Adam, or is he a substitute for Simon?

10. Is Adam too good of a person?

11. When and how is "girl power" introduced in the story?

12. When Adam decides to move to Petersburg, did you think he would be trouble for Carrie?

13. Why is it so hard to believe Simon is bad?

14. How is Richmond, Virginia any different from Jefferson County?

15. Why is it so fascinating for Carrie to ride the train to school?

16. Nadine's "ole man," as he is referred to in the book, becomes Carrie's conscience, yet she never seems to let him in. Why?

17. Simon's fate was something no one saw coming. Do you feel he will rise up again?

18. What kind of business do you think Simon is in, and why was he with Bessie Smith?

19. At what point did Carrie finally become a woman?

20. What is the significance of cranberries to the story?

ABOUT THE AUTHOR

Ruth P. Watson is the author of *Blackberry Days of Summer, An Elderberry Fall* and *Cranberry Winter*. She lives in Atlanta, Georgia, with her husband and son. She divides her time between being a business owner, writer, and educator. She has a master's degree and is currently working on her next novel, *Strawberry Spring*, and a documentary. A musical stageplay, *Blackberry Daze*, is based on her debut novel.

ABOUT THE AUTHOR

If you enjoyed *Cranberry Winter*,
be sure to check out

BLACKBERRY DAYS OF SUMMER

by Ruth P. Watson
AVAILABLE FROM STREBOR BOOKS

CHAPTER 1
CARRIE

Mr. Camm barely waited for Papa to be put in the ground. The next day he slithered into our house, mesmerizing Momma with his poison as she lay down with him. That was when all my troubles started.

I vividly remember the awful day when Papa was summoned to die. It was around two o'clock in the afternoon. The thermometer hanging over the kitchen door read ninety-five degrees, and the gray cotton dress I was wearing clung to my back like molasses to a pancake. Momma sat at the kitchen table gazing blankly out the window. The lines in her face were forged by misfortune and her round chestnut-colored eyes were cloudy with sad tears that trickled down her cocoa cheeks. She blotted her eyes with her hanky, but they continued to leak like a river that had long overflowed.

"Y'all come on in and sit down," she mumbled in a voice so muted I hardly recognized it.

My brothers and I each pulled out a chair and sat down. We were not used to seeing her so broken. Usually she was on her feet handing out orders.

"Why are you crying? What's wrong with ya, Momma?" Carl asked, patting her gently on the shoulder.

Her lips trembled as she said softly, "It's your papa. He done took sick. He been complaining of a headache and now his lips are twisted to one side. He can't even stand up. He ain't doing good."

We glanced at each other with puzzled frowns and waited for someone to figure out what to do. But nobody did.

"What can we do?" Carl asked with the same authority my papa would have used if he'd been feeling well.

"Be there for him, he's gonna need you," Momma said.

When I saw Papa lying there in the bed helpless, with his eyes rolled back in his head, tears welled up in my eyes. Papa was a big black man, over six feet five inches tall, and strong as a horse. He never smoked or drank liquor the way most men wished away their troubles, mistresses, or debts. We all believed his mind and his body were solid, too strong to be ravaged by sickness.

Papa had grown up a free man. His daddy had inherited land from his father, given to him by his master, who felt that good service should be rewarded. When the master was fifty years old, dry and nearly dead from pneumonia, he deeded my grandpa some land for all of his hard labor. Yet, even though Papa owned the land, he cut corners every way he could to pay the taxes. Sometimes the profit from his tobacco crop was only enough to break even. He'd help other farmers on Saturday evenings cut down trees or whatever little he could do, all in an effort to make extra cash. He raised pigs, and no matter how many he hung in the smokehouse, our family was only allowed one ham, which was saved and cooked at Christmas.

When I went into his bedroom and saw him lying there, I fell to my knees and began to pray: *Heavenly Father, who's going to take care of us? We need our papa. Please make him well. Amen.*

Momma was both frightened and saddened by Papa's illness. During his sickness, she sat in the rocking chair beside his bed all night and watched him sleep, massaging her temples with the balls of her thumbs and holding her head back while staring at the ceiling, waiting for a sign. Dark circles cast shadows under her big, beautiful eyes. Her hair was frizzled, unattended to, and stuck to one side of her head. Papa was the love of her life even though she never seemed to know how to respond to his affectionate ways, especially the nights when he would stroke her cheeks as they sat close on the porch watching the lightning bugs and counting the stars. She'd ease away from his attention, and he would only shake his head. To see Momma showing her love for Papa now was a clear message to us all: our world was falling apart.

We kept expecting Papa to stand up, stick his big chest out and head right back to the field, anxious to weed the garden, and see if his seeds were sprouting.

Papa moaned and tossed and turned all night, and then when

he had enough, he closed his eyes. It was half past four in the afternoon, so hot outside that a drop of water would sizzle if it hit the dry, red dirt. Momma hung her head low and covered her eyes. That's when I knew. I cried until my eyes were swollen almost shut. All I could do was grip her shoulders and hold her tight. A part of me died that day with my papa.

Momma cried out, "I'd seen this day coming. It come to me in my dream the night before it happened; he fell right down in the field, arms pointing east and west, and I couldn't revive him. He was too stubborn to slow down and rest, didn't think anybody could work as hard as he could. I begged him the otha mawnin' to stay inside and he stared me straight in the eyes, put on that ole straw hat and walked out the door. You see, Tuesday was da sun's day. He lay right down in da sun and began to die. Sho nuff did."

Carl drove the two mules down to Aunt Bessie's to pick her up. We knew that Momma would need the comfort of her sister. I stood in the frame of her bedroom door and watched her take cash out of an old cigar box she kept under her bed. She handed the crumpled money to the rough-looking white man in bib overalls with red dirt glued under his fingernails who'd come from the undertakers. Afterward, he and a field hand put the casket in the front room and left.

Even before the minister arrived to bless Papa's body, Momma and Bessie went in the kitchen and took out some herbs from the cabinet. They went into the bedroom, where Papa was still lying, washed his body from head to toe, and then rubbed the herbs on him. They dressed him in the only black suit he owned—the one he wore to funerals and church on Sundays.

"Bessie, Lord knows that Robert would want us to be strong,

but it's hard," Momma said, battling back tears. I knew it was tough because crying was a sign of weakness in her mind.

"He looks like he is just sleeping, Mae Lou," Bessie said, buttoning up Papa's suit jacket and staring down at the corpse.

"He's been struggling all of his life with the mighty sun suffering for a long while, and now God got him, no more fighting." Momma said as she folded Papa's hands across his wide chest. Papa died only a few days after his thirty-eighth birthday.

Bessie sat down in the high-back chair Papa used to sit in, and she stared Momma right in the eyes. "How you gonna run the farm without a man around?"

"I don't know."

"You need a man, Mae Lou."

"Everybody needs a man around, but it ain't right to think about that now."

"Well, it's hard when ya all alone," she said, and began to rock as the thought of being alone lingered in the air.

My papa lay in the front room for two days before I decided to talk to him. After everyone went to bed, I lit a candle and took tiny steps down the shadowed gray hallway to his casket, careful not to knock over anything. The floors creaked and the blackness was all over the country at night. Through the window I noticed only a few stars sprinkled across the midnight sky. I reached the front room without anyone hearing me, and the metal hinge in the casket screeched as I opened it. I wasn't afraid of dead people because Momma and Papa said that the dead couldn't hurt you no way.

An eerie feeling crept over me when I glanced down at Papa's stiff body and leathery skin, sunburned almost black. Tears leaked out the corners of my eyes as I leaned over his corpse and began to speak to him. The candlelight cast my moving shadow on the wall, but I still wasn't afraid. I stood sobbing as droplets of my tears lingered on his burial suit.

"Oh, Papa, I'm going to miss you," I whispered. "I'm sorry you had to die, and I know this house will not be the same." I leaned over and kissed his comatose cheek. "I'm going to be okay, though. I'm going to get away from around here and go to college, like you wanted me to do. I promise, I'm going to make you proud."

I said things to Papa that night that I should have said before he passed. After I finished, I felt relieved. I dried my tears with the back of my hands and went back to my room. Somehow, I knew that he had heard me. I knew that Papa didn't want me to cry for him. Aunt Bessie was right, he looked like he was sleeping, free of all labor and pain, a look of peace permanent on his face.

We grieved for over a week before we buried Papa. If the smell of rotten flesh had not gotten unbearable, he probably would have lain in the front room longer. Members of the New Covenant Baptist Church drove their buggies to our house. Papa was on the board of deacons and everyone respected him. Countless folks brought us fried chicken and ham and potato pies.

The day of the funeral was hard for us. Saying good-bye to my father felt like something I treasured had been ripped away from my arms. The deacons arrived at our house early on that Sunday morning. And like the day he died, the sun stood at attention and peeked at us through the clouds. They loaded Papa's body onto a wagon to take to the church a few miles down the road. When they lifted the casket and slid it onto the wagon, I cried out. I'd felt comforted with his stiff body sleeping in the front room. The deacon with the lazy eye told me to be at peace. I went quiet, but snorted back salty tears all the way to the church.

All during the service, Mr. Camm stood close to Momma as if he knew her and Papa. He even offered her his handkerchief, but she didn't have tears. She looked up at him and he grinned, like a man does with a pretty woman. He reached over and softly touched her on the arm. She didn't flinch.

Papa was buried in the cemetery behind the church, like most of his family. He was buried a few feet from his mother. His daddy was buried in the slave cemetery on the plantation. My brothers fought back tears all through the service, yet Momma still didn't cry. I suppose she had done all her crying at home.

Momma stood at the foot of his grave for ten minutes after the service was complete. We were the last people to leave the grave-yard. We even waited until the deacons and the grave attendant had covered Papa's casket with dirt. Then Carl drove us home.

Nobody said a word. Some of the same people who came with us to the church followed us home to celebrate Papa's home- going.

Mr. Camm came, too, though he shouldn't have been there. I frowned at him, unsettled by his walnut-colored skin and dark, beady eyes set deep in his head. I noticed him peering at me, watching my every move, staring openly without blinking. Words don't do justice to how uncomfortable he made me feel.

He had that effect on a lot of people. It was no wonder that so many people wanted him dead.